THE HASTY HANGMAN

THE HASTY HANGMAN

RAY HOGAN

SAGEBRUSH
Large Print Westerns

First published in Great Britain by Mews Books
First published in the United States by Ace Books

Published in Large Print 2005 by ISIS Publishing Ltd,
7 Centremead, Osney Mead, Oxford OX2 0ES
United Kingdom
by arrangement with
Golden West Literary Agency

British Library Cataloguing in Publication Data
Hogan, Ray, 1908–
   The hasty hangman. – Large print ed. –
   (Sagebrush western series)
   1. Impersonation – Fiction
   2. Western stories
   3. Large type books
   I. Title
   813.5'4 [F]

ISBN 0–7531–7295–X (hb)

Printed and bound by Antony Rowe, Chippenham

CAST OF CHARACTERS

BEN COE
He risked his life to save an outlaw for death.

TOM KILGORE
Because he started to do the right thing, he couldn't finish it.

TURK DURET
This skunk did what he wanted and made other men pay for his crimes.

LAURIE BRACKEN
Loving the man everyone else hated was not the smartest thing for this girl to do.

TODD BRACKEN
The hate that clouded his mind caused him to defeat his own purposes.

C. J. PRESTON
Because he was a thief himself, when he was robbed he was ruined.

CHAPTER
ONE

Take the place of a man condemned to die!

Ben Coe, three weeks' growth of black beard masking his hard face, pulled to a halt on the outskirts of Salvation and stared moodily at the brightly lit, jammed street. That was what Kilgore's letter had said they wanted him to do. And Tom Kilgore, the United States marshal for that area was the one who called the shots.

There had been but little more information contained in the summons. Explanation would come later, the lawman had stated. Coe was to report in Salvation, arriving unseen and unnoticed by anyone. The importance of that could not be overstressed. He was to present himself immediately at the home of Judge Frank Abraham.

He was to be there on the fourteenth. The trial of the killer, Turk Duret, was set for the morning of the fifteenth and he had just made it. This was now the night of the fourteenth.

Now the long and lonely ride from Kansas was over. The noise and activity of the surging town were a welcome change and most inviting. For several minutes he sat there in the darkness, watching and listening, a wide-shouldered, slightly hunched figure on a weary buckskin horse. It would appear that almost the whole Territory had turned up to witness the trial of Turk Duret. He must be a man well hated, Ben thought as he scratched idly at a scar tracing along his neck. It was an old habit of his, stroking that seared, white bullet path when he was concerned or thinking deeply. What could Duret have done to warrant such attention? Something more than the usual murder, undoubtedly.

He stirred. The sound of approaching horses coming to him through the warm, soft night. They were coming up the trail he had just covered. Quietly, he drifted back into the thick brush, a dozen feet to his left. He was remembering Kilgore's orders about remaining unseen.

He waited out the moments while the riders, two slouching cowboys on range-worn horses, came into view. They drew alongside and passed. More customers for Duret's trial, he guessed. Kilgore and the local lawmen would likely have their hands full. He had a moment's wish that he, too, might ride into town. It had been a dry, dusty day and the July heat had been a fierce, withering blast since sunup. A cool glass of beer certainly would taste good. But he would have to forget that. Perhaps the judge could provide something wet and cold when he checked in.

He reckoned he should be getting there. Kilgore and the judge probably were beginning to worry about his arrival. He reached for the star pinned inside his shirt pocket. Better get it out of sight, just in case. For a moment he stared at its dully shining surface, the worn black letters proclaiming him a deputy U. S. marshal

2

barely legible. This would be the first time in almost five years he would not be wearing his badge. With a faint sigh he half turned, and taking the near empty sack of coffee from the left saddlebag, he buried the star in its depths. It would be safely hidden there.

Touching the buckskin lightly with his spurs, he cut across the trail and headed for the west side of town. As they moved deeper into the brush, Coe half rose in the stirrups, having one more look at the teeming town. His last good one, most likely, for tomorrow, if his guesses were correct, he would be seeing it through the barred window of a cell. And he would be the most hated man in the Territory.

A woman's anguished cry suddenly shattered the stillness of the grove. It seemed to come from the trail, back where he had been. Coe halted, listening. The cry reached him again.

"Help! Please somebody, help!"

The words ended in a muffled sob. He wheeled the buckskin about sharply and drove hard for the sound.

In only moments he was on the scene. The two cowboys he had seen earlier had dismounted and were standing before a girl whom they had backed against a thick cottonwood tree. One of the pair was holding the girl and had her arms pinned back. The other, a bottle in his hand, was attempting to force a drink down her throat. The girl was twisting about and struggling wildly to break free. Her dark hair had come loose and was now flowing about her shoulders. Her face, clean cut as a cameo in the pale light, reflected her stark fear.

"Go away! Leave me alone. Please, leave me alone!"

"You hear that, Keno?" the man with the bottle asked, pausing. "Wants us to leave her be!"

"She sure ain't very sociable. Go on, give her a drink or two. Maybe that'll sweeten her up a mite."

Coe, jerking his hat lower over his face, pointed the buckskin straight for the two cowboys. The pound of the horse's hooves brought them unsteadily around. The one holding the girl let his hands fall away and stepped back. The other, bottle still in his fingers, wheeled to make a stand. Coe's down-sledging fist caught him high on the cheek and knocked him to the ground.

From the corner of his eye Ben saw the first rider reach for his pistol.

"Don't draw!" he warned, bringing the buckskin around in a tight circle. "Make a move to pull that gun and I'll put a bullet in your belly!"

The cowboy hastily lifted his hands. "We didn't mean no harm," he muttered thickly. "Was just havin' us a little fun."

"Wrong kind of fun, seems to me," Coe said coldly. "Now load your partner onto his horse and ride out of here. You come back this way again and I'll use this gun. That clear?"

"It's clear," the man grumbled. He turned to his friend, now stirring dazedly on the ground. Taking him under the armpits, he managed to get him on his feet and then into his saddle. Mounting up himself, he started off down the trail, leading the other horse.

4

Keeping his face tipped, Coe glanced at the girl. She was standing in the open, her eyes upon him. She was pretty, he noted, and well fashioned.

"You all right?" he asked.

She nodded. "Thank you for coming when I yelled. They slipped up on me."

"Not a very good idea, you being out here alone like this, Miss —"

"Bracken. Laurie Bracken."

"Miss Bracken. Probably be a lot of rough characters passing this way tonight. You live around close?"

"We have a camp down near the river. My father and brother and a couple of friends. We're here for the trial." She paused, adding a moment later, "It's only a little ways and I could make some fresh coffee if you would like."

"I'm obliged," Coe said, wishing he might accept the invitation. But he was already late. "Got to be pushing on. Some business that has to be tended to. I'll remember that offer though, if it's all right with you."

He could see her smile. "The offer stands," she said.

"Fine. Now, I think you ought to be getting back to your camp. Don't think that pair will come back but there will be others."

"I'm going," she said, turning off the trail. "Thank you again."

"My pleasure," Coe replied courteously and watched her disappear into the darkness.

CHAPTER
TWO

Coe located Abraham's ornate residence and drew to a halt in the tamarack windbreak bordering its south side. Light shone through a lower-floor window.

Movement beyond the window brought his attention up sharply. The figure of a man crossed in front of the green-shaded lamp. That would be Abraham, most likely.

There was a second man in the well furnished parlor. He, and the one who had moved across the window, sat at opposite sides of a heavily scrolled and carved table playing some sort of card game in which neither seemed greatly interested.

The one on the left was Tom Kilgore, a huge man, somewhere in his early fifties.

The other man would be Frank Abraham, the judge. He was older, well up in his sixties. He wore his snow white hair shoulder length and his spade beard, also white, set off his florid, narrow features. A pair of steel-rimmed spectacles sat near the tip of his hawk beak nose and despite the warmness of the night, his shirt was cuffed at the wrists and closed at the collar with a black string tie.

6

That the pair were impatiently awaiting him Coe realized when he saw Kilgore glance at his turnip watch for the third or fourth time in as many minutes. He moved in closer to the window, taking care not to silhouette himself against the block of light. He tapped lightly upon the glass. Kilgore flicked a glance at the window. The judge did not move. After a few moments the marshal rose and casually walked to a door facing him. A short time later Coe heard a sound in the shrubbery alongside the house.

Kilgore's deep voice asked, "Coe?"

"Right."

"Good," the lawman grunted. "Figured it was, but had to be sure. Come back this way."

Ben ducked below the ledge of the window and moved to where the marshal waited. He accepted Kilgore's strong handshake and followed him then to a rear door. Once inside the house, they crossed a room, a kitchen, and entered a short hallway.

"That shade down, Frank?"

"It's down. Come on in."

Coe trailed Kilgore into the room where the jurist waited. The lawman made his introductions and Abraham at once asked, "You sure nobody saw you come here, Coe?"

Ben nodded. "Met nobody this side of the town. Had a little ruckus when I first rode in. Only people I've seen closer than a hundred yards."

Kilgore came alert at once. "That ruckus — anybody get a good look at you?"

Coe said, "No. Too dark for them to see much. Kept my face down anyway."

"What happened?"

"Couple of drunks trying to rough up a girl, that's all."

Kilgore again displayed his relief. He turned to the table. "Ticklish business," he murmured. "You cut things a little fine. Expected you a couple of days ago."

Coe shrugged. "Your letter took a bit of time running me down. Came fast as I could when I read it. What's this all about, anyway?"

Abraham broke in. "Expect you're a little dry and hungry. Can't do you any good on the food end. I live here alone and do my eating in town. But I've got plenty of good, cold water. Marshal can fix you up with a meal after you're safely locked in a cell."

The judge moved to a richly carved, ebony black sideboard. He poured a tall glass of water from a crockery pitcher.

"Sit yourself down, son," he said, handing the glass to Ben. "Make yourself comfortable and we'll explain."

Coe settled himself into one of the deep, leather-covered chairs.

"Don't like to ask a man to do what we've got in mind," Kilgore said, taking his place at the table, "but we've got us a situation that calls for some unusual methods."

"First time anybody ever asked me to take the place of a man about to get hung," Coe said with a wry grin.

"Just about what it amounts to," Abraham admitted, "short of the hanging part, of course."

"This Turk Duret must be a mighty important prisoner," Ben said.

"More than you'd guess," Kilgore answered immediately. "A lot rides on that jasper getting properly hung. That's why I sent for you. Can't have anything go wrong."

"Why can't you just hang him here, like you would any other killer?"

"Job's got to be done in Capital City. That's the Governor's orders. Wants it done there on the scaffold inside the prison yard to prove a point. And Capital City is a two day ride from here."

Coe frowned, considering the words. "You figure to have trouble getting him there, that it?"

"Plumb sure of it!" Kilgore said heatedly. "The way people all over this Territory are feeling, we're bound to have plenty of hell, right from the start."

"Which means we'll have the same hell getting me there in his place."

Kilgore nodded. He let his eyes meet those of the deputy marshal. "Like I said in my letter, Coe, you've got a choice. You don't have to go through with it. It'll be risky. Could get us both killed. But there'll be no hard feelings if you want to pull out."

"Reckon a man dies when his time comes," Coe said, taking a deep drag of his cigarette. "Don't figure my time has showed up yet."

"Good," Kilgore answered with a hard grin. He nodded to Abraham. "Told you he was our man, Frank."

9

Abraham said, "I'm sure of it. But I still think he ought to hear the whole thing before making up his mind."

Kilgore laid his thick arms across the table and rested himself on his elbows. "Turk Duret was serving a twenty year term in Capital City for a stage robbery. He did about two years of it and broke out. We don't know yet just how he managed it for the Territorial prison is a hard place to get out of if they don't want you to leave. Anyway, he pulled it off. And he killed two guards doing it, one of them needlessly.

"We lost him completely for about a week. Then he showed up in a town south of here. Walked into a bank, shot down the clerk and a rancher who was there doing some business, and walked back out with about thirty thousand dollars. Naturally, the shots attracted the town marshal and some other men down the street and when he stepped into the open, they caught on quick what was going on and started blasting at him.

"There was a woman, not much more than a girl actually, with her baby, sitting in a buckboard right next to the bank. Duret saw he was outnumbered so he jumped up into the buckboard and grabbed the baby. Everybody stopped shooting then, of course. Duret, using the girl and her baby as shields, drove out of town."

Coe revolved the words about in his mind. No wonder Turk Duret was so important! Four murders plus the crimes that had sent him into a prison cell in the first place. And topping those off with the kidnapping of a mother and her child!

"What happened next?"

"Worst thing of all, I guess you would say," Frank Abraham replied in a low voice. "He drove the buckboard into the hills, taking the girl and her child with him. He holed up with them in a cave. Both of them died." The jurist halted, studying the heavy ring on his left hand. "The baby from neglect and starvation, the woman from mistreatment. Nobody," he added slowly, "will ever know the hell that poor girl went through at the hands of that brute."

Coe felt his scalp crawl. Duret was more than a killer — he was a fiend, a depraved monster. The reason for the huge crowd gathered in Salvation for the trial was clear now.

"How long did he hold them in that cave?" he asked.

"Almost two weeks."

"Two weeks," Coe echoed. "Looks like he would have needed supplies. Wonder somebody didn't spot him when he went after them."

"Just what did happen," Kilgore explained. "Reckon he must have had that cave all set up beforehand. Probably was what he was doing in that week when he dropped out of sight. But his store of grub finally did run out and he went to a little settlement on the far side of the mountain where he figured he wouldn't be recognized, I guess. Only thing, the storekeeper got suspicious and put the sheriff on his trail. They hemmed him up and took him without firing a shot."

"Girl and baby dead by then?"

Kilgore nodded. "Doc says he figures the baby died the first week. Girl had been dead only a couple of days."

Coe shook his head. "What gets into a man and makes him do things like that? I can understand robbery and maybe a killing during an argument. But to take a woman and treat her that way or let a baby die — hard to believe any man could do it!"

"Lucky thing there are not many Durets in this world," Abraham said. "Usually you find some good in the worst criminal, but this Duret, well, I don't believe there is one, single spark of decency in him."

Coe snuffed out his cigarette. "Can't say as I'm going to much enjoy being him, even if it is for just a short time. One thing I am wondering — why me? Must be plenty of men closer than Kansas you could have called in."

"Maybe so," Kilgore said promptly, "but we can't take any chances. You're a stranger around here, for one thing. Nobody ever saw you before. Anyway, we're hoping that's true."

Coe shrugged. "Might be a couple of drifters out there in town that have been up Kansas way. Doubt if they would recognize me, however. This beard makes for a good mask," he added, fingering the stiff growth covering his chin and the sides of his face.

"You're about the same build as Duret," Kilgore went on. "You see, nobody around here ever really saw Duret up close, either."

Coe frowned. "Not even the girl's folks? Her husband?"

"None of them saw Duret. What they and all the rest of the people around here don't know, is that Duret's already been tried in court and sentenced to hang. It was done in secret, at a town near the border."

That made little sense to Coe. "Then why the trial tomorrow?"

"One reason only, we want people believing you are Turk Duret. This trial, or hearing, is purely to set up our plan. If the crowd or anybody in it gets ideas about handing out their own brand of lynch law, it will be you they'll be after."

"And the real Duret?"

"Marcelino Baca, the sheriff, will be taking him to Capital City by a different road."

Coe studied the high ceiling of the room. The plan was an ingenious one, but dangerous for him. "Where's Duret now?"

"Right here in town. In jail."

Coe's attention dropped quickly to Kilgore. The big lawman grinned. "Locked up on a robbery charge. At least, that's what we're letting everybody think."

"But, isn't he liable to start shooting off his mouth? Don't you think he might tell somebody he's Turk Duret?"

Kilgore cast a sidelong glance at Judge Abraham. "Reckon he's the only prisoner in history that the law has kept dead drunk ever since he was thrown into a cell."

"Who all is in on the plan?"

"Four people. You, the judge, myself and Marcelino Baca, the sheriff. No more."

13

"Good," Coe said. "Less chance of a slip-up if there's only a few knowing about it."

Judge Abraham nodded. He leaned forward, looked more closely at Ben. "From what you just said, I take it you're agreeable to helping us?"

Coe said, "Sure. I thought you understood that. I was just getting filled in on the details. What's the next move?"

"I'll ride in with you," Kilgore replied. "Just like I was just hitting town. Nobody knows I'm around, either. Been holed up in this damned house for three days. Sure will be good to get outside and moving around."

Abraham gave him a sardonic glance. "You better be appreciating all this privacy while you got a chance. Once you show up in town with Turk Duret in tow, there'll be somebody breathing down your neck every minute. You ready to go?"

"Guess you're right about the privacy," the older lawman said. "Reckon we're ready to make our move."

"I'll go get Marcelino and a couple of deputies. Got to escort our prisoner in style."

"Style, the devil!" Kilgore snorted. "If we don't have an escort, we won't have a prisoner long! Tell the sheriff he better bring three men with him."

"Three it is," Abraham said and passed through the doorway.

CHAPTER
THREE

"Won't take him long," Kilgore said as Abraham's footsteps faded down the brick walk. "We'd better be getting set."

He took a pair of handcuffs from his pocket and tossed them to Coe. "Put these on. I'll go round up the horses. Idea is to make everybody think we just rode in."

Ben snapped the steel cuffs about his wrists. "Left my buckskin in the tamaracks."

Kilgore nodded and left the room. Coe settled back again in the chair. The house was quiet, warm. It had been a long, hard ride down from Kansas and now, just sitting in the deeply-cushioned chair, thinking of nothing, was good.

Kilgore was back a few minutes later. He came through the doorway brushing his hands. "Now, that part's done. Buckskin of yours looks pretty much beat. May have to dig up another horse for you to ride."

"When do you figure to start for Capital City?"

"Trial is tomorrow morning. Everything goes right, we'll pull out the next day."

"The buckskin will be all right by then. Give him a couple of nights' rest and some grain, that's all. He's strong. Besides, I'd rather have my own horse under me in case we run into trouble."

"Know what you mean," Kilgore said, nodding. "And we sure might have plenty of it."

"Anybody in particular?"

"Look for a lot of hollering from everybody when they learn Duret's to be hung in Capital City. People don't trust politicians much in this territory and they're going to want to do their own hanging right here in their own back yard. And the girl's own kinfolks sure ain't going to like it. Add to that C. J. Preston's angle and you get a fair picture of what's ahead for us."

"C. J. Preston — who's he?" Coe wanted to know.

"The owner of the bank Duret held up. That thirty thousand dollars was never found. Duret hid it somewhere."

"And you figure Preston will try to get to Duret and make him talk?"

Kilgore nodded. "He'll try anything to get that money back." The lawman paused, listened. "Sounds like the escort has arrived. Just keep quiet. No need for you to do any talking."

Coe signaled his understanding. Noting then the gunbelt still about Ben's waist, Kilgore stepped forward quickly, unbuckled it and tossed it into a chair. He grinned at Coe.

"Dang near forgot that! Where's your badge?"

"In my saddlebags. Hid in a sack of coffee."

"Good," Kilgore said. There was a knock at the front door. He moved toward it. Pausing there, he ran his gaze over Coe once more, giving him a final inspection. Satisfied all was ready, he swung back the panel.

"Evening, Sheriff, boys," he said, stepping back to admit the men.

Marcelino Baca, the sheriff, was a large man, almost the size of Kilgore. He had the dark hair and eyes, the heavy features, the broad, white teeth of the Spanish. He nodded, flicked Coe with a cool glance as he entered the room. Only his eyes conveyed a greeting to Ben Coe.

The man behind him wore a deputy's star. He was a tall blond, perhaps thirty years old. He carried a carbine in his hands as did the two special deputies who were at his heels. They ranged up before Coe, their features portraying their disgust and hatred for Turk Duret.

Kilgore shook hands all around. To Baca he said, "How's that crowd?"

"Not too wild yet," the sheriff replied. "Mostly getting liquored up tonight. Don't think we'll have much trouble."

Kilgore said, "Good. Let's get him down there and locked up. Suspect he's a mite hungry, same as I am."

The blond deputy snorted. "Let him stay hungry! I had my way, he could starve!"

Baca's big shape wheeled on the man swiftly. "You aren't having your way, Halvers! You get this straight. This man might be a killer but he's going to have protection as long as he's in my custody. Remember that! Makes no difference how you feel about him, he's got the protection of the law. Understand?"

Halvers' eyes were fastened to Coe's. "I understand," he replied in a low voice. "But I'm not saying I like it."

"I don't care whether you like it or not," Baca said softly. "You just do what you're told. Any time you decide you don't want to, just lay that badge on my desk and get out. I won't have any deputies around who figure the law doesn't work both sides of the table." He lifted his attention to the other lawmen. "How do you boys feel about it?"

"You're ramroddin' this deal, Sheriff," one said. "Whatever you say goes with me."

"Me, too," the other added.

"Good," Baca said. "We're ready to go, Marshal. You and your prisoner will ride in the center. We'll space out around you. Case of trouble," he added to his deputies, "we'll do no shooting unless forced to. Use your rifles as clubs."

Kilgore took Coe by the arm and guided him to the doorway. Baca and his men fell in behind. They entered the yard where the horses stood at the hitching rail. Kilgore assisted Coe to mount and swung onto his own animal. With Baca and Halvers slightly ahead and the remaining two lawmen at the rear, they left Abraham's and started for town.

It was a short ride. Down a dark and quiet lane, deep in shadows, to the main street of Salvation, ablaze with lamplight and pulsing with an overload of humanity. They breasted it head on, Halvers and Marcelino Baca clearing the way before them with shouts and drawn guns. The crowd parted reluctantly. Coe felt the eyes of many upon him, sensed the hatred they bore. It would

18

have been better for them to have arrived by a less conspicuous route.

Yet he knew there was sound reasoning behind Kilgore's movements. He must establish Coe as Turk Duret in the minds of all who were in Salvation. This was the best way to accomplish that. Coe flinched as a small rock, thrown from the depths of the gathering, struck his arm and glanced off. A man, somewhat unsteady from drink, lurched in from the side, clawing at Ben's leg. One of the deputies moved up quickly, placed his foot against the drunk's shoulder and sent him sprawling back into the crowd.

"Keep back! Keep back!" Baca shouted. "Don't want anybody hurt here tonight!"

The shuffling, swaying throng had stirred the loose dust into thick, billowing clouds. It hung now over the street in a choking, yellowish blanket.

Their progress was slow but they pushed on. More hands reached for Coe but Halvers had dropped back to his side and crowded them out. Kilgore, on the left, gave him protection at that point. Ben glanced ahead. He was bathed with sweat and he would be glad when the trip was over. The jail was now only a dozen yards distant. A few more minutes and they would be safely inside. It was an uncomfortable feeling, having several hundred persons glaring up at him, all thirsting for his blood.

Baca pulled to a stop at the rail at the rear of the jail. Dismounting, he hurried to unlock the door. Kilgore and Coe followed him to the inside. Closing the thick

19

panel and dropping the bar into place, the sheriff mopped at his swarthy face and grinned.

"A little close, eh, *amigo*?"

"Too close," Kilgore grunted, shoving his pistol back into its holster. "Thought for a minute I'd made a bad guess. But I think we've convinced them. Sorry we had to put you through that," he added, looking at Coe.

Ben shook his head. "Mighty glad this jail wasn't at the other end of the street."

He walked deeper into the room, halted in front of the two cells. One was empty, the other contained a man. He was stretched out full length on the cot, sound asleep, his mouth blared open, one arm and leg hanging off and touching the floor. A half empty whiskey bottle was nearby.

Coe glanced to Kilgore. "Duret?"

The marshal said, "That's him. A real pretty sight!" He hesitated as someone knocked at the door. "Reckon you'd better be getting inside that cell. Halvers and the others will be coming in."

Ben walked into the barred cubicle. He moved to the cot and sat down, watching as Kilgore slammed the heavy cell door and snapped the lock. After a time there was a second rapping on the door. Baca, drawing his pistol, stepped forward and opened it cautiously. It was Halvers.

"Left the other boys to keep an eye on things," he said, pushing inside. "Most of the crowd's moved on. Only ones still hanging around are the Bracken bunch."

Bracken. The name sounded vaguely familiar to Ben Coe. He resolved it through his mind, trying to recall where he had heard it before.

"We'll have trouble with them," Baca said, wagging his head.

"Can't blame them much!" Halvers declared, glaring hotly at Coe. "Man do to my wife and baby what he did to Todd Bracken's, I'd be honin' for a chance to even the score, too!"

Bracken — *Laurie Bracken*! It came to Ben Coe in a sudden burst of remembrance. A heaviness settled down upon him. Sometimes nothing worked out right for a man!

CHAPTER
FOUR

Ben Coe was awake with the sunrise. He had slept well despite the precariousness of his position and for the first time in weeks he felt rested.

It was around seven o'clock, and the sheriff, followed by Deputy Halvers, entered. The lawman carried a tray.

"Get back away from the door," Halvers ordered, coming to a halt in front of Coe's cell.

Ben sat down on his cot. The deputy opened the door and cautiously slid the tray inside. "If that ain't enough, just let me know," he said. "We always give a man a big feed before we hang him."

Standing behind Halvers, Marcelino Baca winked broadly at Coe.

It was eight-thirty when Tom Kilgore made his appearance. He greeted the other lawmen, cast a sidelong glance at Coe and studied the motionless figure of Turk Duret for a moment. He then sat down in a chair next to the sheriff's desk.

"Crowd's already gathering at the courthouse. Expect we'd better be getting our prisoner over there."

Baca nodded. He turned to Halvers. "Carl, walk down the alley and see how things look. We'll take Duret the back way. No sense tempting anybody now."

The blond deputy left. Kilgore's glance swung to the other two lawmen. "How about you two taking a little stroll down the street. See what the talk is. Might hear something we ought to know. But be back in ten minutes."

The pair moved out at once. When the door had closed behind them, Kilgore arose, and taking the cell keys, released Coe. Handing the deputy his handcuffs to place about his wrists, he said, "Figured we ought to get things straight. Now, about this trial. It will be short. We'll all go in the courtroom. The judge will have the charge read and ask you how you plead. All you say is, guilty. He'll pass sentence and after that we'll get up and leave. Crowd gets a little wild, we'll stay a bit in the anteroom behind the courtroom until things quiet down. Then we'll come back here."

"Here comes Halvers," Baca announced. He stepped to the rear of the room and lifted the bar lock. The deputy entered. He gave Coe a swift appraisal.

"Nobody along the alley," he said. "What can't get inside the courthouse is standin' out in front. We won't have a better chance to get him there."

"We ought to wait for the other boys," Kilgore said. "Should be back by now."

Baca moved to the front entrance. Opening it, he glanced down the street. He called to the two men who were just returning. In a moment they were inside.

"Same orders as last night," Baca said then. "No shooting unless it's absolutely necessary. Use your rifles like clubs. But the prisoner gets *there* safely and gets *back* the same way. Am I making myself clear?"

The deputies nodded. The sheriff walked to the rear and checked the alleyway once more. "All clear," he said and stepped outside. Coe, Kilgore and the others filed out. Baca stopped the last man.

"Turner, you better stay here with the other prisoner. He might have a friend that would try and break him out. Just keep the doors locked and don't let anybody in to talk to him."

Turner started to protest then, shrugging, turned back into the jail. Carl Halvers called to him.

"Don't fret yourself, Bob. This won't take long. And you can sure watch the hanging."

They passed quickly down the narrow passageway and entered the rear of the frame courthouse without incident. A small fringe of the crowd saw them as they crossed the street and a shout went up but there was no move to intercept them. At the moment it appeared everyone was more interested in getting inside the building to witness the affair than in taking the law in their own hands.

They walked along a short, dark hallway and stopped at a door. Kilgore rapped twice upon it. Coe heard its lock grate and watched it swing back. It led into the main courtroom.

It was packed with noisy spectators and already breathlessly hot. A shout went up when they made their appearance. Kilgore motioned Coe to one of the dozen or so chairs placed in the small area separated from the spectators by a belt-high railing. Halvers and the other deputy took up a position directly behind him. Kilgore settled down in a place at the right and near the judge's table.

Smoke hung from the ceiling in boiling, shifting clouds and the stench from sweaty, unwashed bodies was like a thick blanket in the room bulging with four times its intended capacity.

Ben allowed his gaze to slide over the room. It was jammed tight, even the aisles having disappeared. He saw Laurie Bracken then. She was sitting in the first row beyond the railing. The younger man on her left would be her brother, the husband of the woman Turk Duret murdered. The older man likely was her father. All three were watching him with a cold, unforgiving hatred.

"Everybody get up!" The man who had been posted at the locked door yelled his command.

There was a general clatter of confusion as those who were seated arose. Judge Abraham entered, walked to his bench. He glanced out over the crowd, nodded to the bailiff and sat down.

"Hear ye!" the bailiff shouted, facing the assembly. "Everybody quiet now. This here court of Judge Frank Abraham is in session. Let's don't have no more of this racket!"

Abraham's frosty brows pulled down into a firm line. He let his hard eyes again sweep the room.

"Let this be understood," he said in a cold voice, "this is a court of law and it will be respected as such. Any unseemly behavior on the part of any man or woman will call for immediate action on my part. I will clear this courtroom instantly."

There was a complete silence on the heels of his words. He allowed it to ride for a full minute and then turned his attention to the bailiff.

"I do not see the prosecutor or the court clerk present. Where are they?"

Before the deputy could make a reply, a voice shouted from the audience: "You won't be needin' them, Judge! We all know this Duret's guilty. Why you botherin' to trial him, anyway?"

Abraham's florid face colored a deeper shade. He rapped on the table sharply. "Deputy!" he shouted, half rising. "Get that man out of this courtroom!"

One of the lawmen standing near the entrance hurriedly shouldered his way through the pack to the offender. Clamping his hand upon the man's arm, he hustled him out.

"The next outburst like that and everybody will leave," Abraham warned. "I'll have no such foolishness."

Two men entered the room from the side door at that point. A balding, well dressed man with a sheaf of papers under his arm; a small, thin, shabby individual with a face like a ferret. The first halted before the judge.

"Mr. Allison," Abraham said, recognizing the man.

"I apologize for being late, your honor. Our clerk, Mr. Conley, misplaced some of the necessary papers. We were delayed while he located them."

Abraham threw a withering look at the small man. He nodded to the prosecutor. "Very well, Mr. Allison. I assume we are now ready to proceed."

Allison said, "Yes, your honor," and moved to an empty chair next to the court clerk.

The judge cleared his throat. "I would like to have it understood that this is not a trial. It is a hearing at which the prisoner will learn of the charges placed against him. He will then have the opportunity for lodging his plea."

There was a murmur through the audience. Abraham pounded on his table. He swung his attention to Kilgore. "Is the prisoner represented by counsel?"

The marshal stood up. "No, your honor. The prisoner says he doesn't want a lawyer."

Abraham nodded. His gaze came back to Conley. "The clerk will read the charge."

Harvey Conley got nervously to his feet. Adjusting his silver-rimmed glasses, he fumbled a moment with the papers in his hands and then began.

"That the accused, Turk Duret, who, while serving a term in the Territorial prison did break out and escape and kill two guards, in so doing. That he later robbed the Canyon County Bank at Junction City of the sum of thirty thousand dollars and in the doing did kill Oscar Brewer and James Mattingly. And while further escaping he did seize, kidnap and carry off as hostages one Molly Bracken and her child, Christine Bracken, both of whom died while being held captive in a cave where the accused was hiding."

Conley stopped. He mopped at the beaded sweat on his forehead and peered over his spectacles at the judge. "That's it, your honor."

"Prisoner, how do you plead? Guilty or not guilty to the charges made?" the judge asked.

Ben Coe rose slowly. Keeping his head tipped down, he said, "Guilty."

There was no sound in the breathlessly hot room. Outside, in the street, the faint rumble of voices could be heard.

Abraham said, "Guilty of all charges?"

The prisoner nodded and sank back into his chair. A man in the back of the room turned and pushed his way through the doorway, his voice shouting the news to those in the street. Abraham studied the backs of his heavily veined hands. He was apparently framing his next pronouncement.

"In that case," he began, his voice stentorian, "I have but one more duty to perform. To declare sentence. Are you ready, Turk Duret?"

Ben Coe again nodded.

"Then stand up."

Coe pulled himself upright, his tall, wide-shouldered frame outlining darkly against the morning sunlight.

"Since you plead guilty to all charges, it will not be necessary to hold a trial by jury. I, therefore, sentence you to death, Turk Duret, for your crimes. You will be hanged by the neck until you are dead and I will ask God to have mercy on your soul. This sentence will be carried out four days from today on the gallows in the yard of the Territorial prison in Capital City."

There was a long moment of stunned silence. Then sudden, wild yells of disappointment ripped through the quiet. Several men leaped to their feet, their chairs

28

overturning and clattering loudly to the floor. Cries of *No! No!* echoed through the crowd. Abraham began to pound on his desk with his gavel. Kilgore came to his feet, his hand resting on his gun while Sheriff Baca, who had been standing sentry at the hall door, moved up beside his deputies, a shotgun cradled in his arms.

"You ain't gettin' away with that, Judge!" a man in the front row shouted. "He'll never hang if you send him up there!"

"You bet he won't!" another voice agreed. "He'll cook himself up a deal with them politicians. He'll tell them where the money's hid and they'll turn him loose!"

The courtroom was bedlam. Abraham rapped on his bench but the sound went unheeded. The judge motioned to Kilgore and when the marshal had stepped to his side, he said something to him. The lawman drew his pistol and fired it into the floor. The shocking blast in the small area brought an immediate quiet.

Abraham held a letter over his head and waved it. "It's not necessary that I explain the actions of this court," he stated, "but in this instance I shall do so. I will tell you why the sentence of Turk Duret must be carried out in Capital City."

He waited until the murmur of voices had again ceased. He began, "This letter is from the Governor. It directs me, upon finding Duret guilty and sentencing him to be hanged, to deliver him to the prison authorities in Capital City for execution. No, wait —" he added hurriedly as the protests started anew.

"The Governor continues: 'Outlaws in this Territory have been having their way for years. They have flaunted our laws, ridiculed our lawmen and done pretty well as they pleased. The public execution in the prison yard of an outlaw as famous as Turk Duret will prove to all the day of the outlaw is over. It will serve as a lesson and a warning to all others of like calibre that this Territory is no longer a refuge for killers and wanted men. It will prove that, at last, we have a strong law, one big enough and able enough to cope with and punish the Turk Durets.'"

"Nothin' but a lot of talk!" a voice cried, almost before the jurist had concluded. "Just a way of gettin' Duret out of our hands so's they can turn him loose."

"He won't be turned loose," Kilgore said flatly.

"He got loose before, didn't he?" the speaker countered. "Man ain't supposed to escape from the pen but he sure did. I figure he had a little help."

Ben Coe was watching Kilgore closely, awaiting instructions from him. The crowd had turned from one of almost festive mood to one of sullen anger bordering on violence. It would take very little to incite them to mob action.

"That's just what'll happen again! He'll tell them where he hid Preston's money and next thing we'll be hearin' is that he escaped!"

Kilgore half swung about to face Baca. "Better get the prisoner out of here, Sheriff. Take him into that anteroom. Lock the door. I'll join you soon as I can get the courtroom cleared."

"Look out!" Halvers yelled.

Coe had a fleeting glimpse of Todd Bracken's shape lunging over the railing at him. He tried to duck away

30

but he was too late. Bracken struck him head on, the force of it carrying him over backwards to the floor. With his hands manacled Coe could do nothing to defend himself. He sought to roll away. Bracken's fingers closed about his throat. He felt the man's knees dig into his back, pinning him down.

The room was a madhouse as spectators surged forward, yelling encouragement and advice to Bracken, seeking to get in their own blows. The sharp toe of a boot drove into Coe's ribs. His face slammed into the floor as someone struck the back of his head. Feet were churning about him, stepping on him, colliding with his body. A gun exploded again but it seemed to have little effect.

The fingers about his throat suddenly slackened their pressure; the knees left his back. Twisting about, he looked upward. Tom Kilgore was standing straddle-legged over him. He had pulled Todd Bracken off him. At the same moment Coe saw what had happened, the big lawman had taken Bracken by the shoulders and hurled him straight into the crowd.

Kilgore bent swiftly. "You all right?"

Coe said, "Out of wind, about all."

The marshal helped him to his feet. Reaching out, Kilgore laid his hand on Marcelino Baca's wrist. The sheriff, standing beside his deputies, keeping the crowd at bay with slow, sweeping movements of their guns, swung about.

"Your chance," Kilgore said. "Get him into that back room and lock the door. We'll clear out this bunch and join you in a few minutes."

CHAPTER
FIVE

They reached the anteroom without incident.

Entering, Baca was about to turn the lock behind them when Abraham and the court clerk, Harvey Conley, who scurried along at the heels of the jurist with a fistful of papers clutched in his hands, hastened to be admitted. The clerk settled down at once at a low table and began to work over his papers while the rest found chairs.

It was a full half hour before Kilgore and the two deputies had dispersed the restless crowd and knocked at the door. The small quarters, often referred to by the judge as his "chambers", were stifling with its dead, dry air and by the time the lawmen arrived, those who waited were sweating freely.

Kilgore, hands on hips, halted in the center of the room. His face was taut and he showed the strain of the past minutes. "Hard to keep somebody from getting hurt in a deal like that," he said. "Some people are just plain damn fools."

"Crowd is plenty worked up," Halvers observed.

Abraham glanced at the marshal. A wry smile twisted his mouth. "Think you can keep Duret alive for a public hanging, Tom?"

Kilgore shrugged. "Not thinking about it, just figuring on doing it."

"You'll never leave town with him," Halvers said. "That's a mean mob out there. Man!" he added, "I never thought one man could make so many people hate him!"

Kilgore was not listening. "Might have been better if we'd rushed him straight back to jail. Got him there before the crowd got out of the building."

Baca turned to one of the deputies. "Take a look down the alley, Cal. See if there's anybody hanging around."

The deputy left the room. Abraham asked, "When you figure to leave with him, Marshal?"

"Daylight, tomorrow morning."

"Means you'll spend the rest of this day and tonight here. You think that's smart?"

"No choice. Got to get things set. And I sure don't want to pull out with that crowd the way it is now. Wouldn't get a half a mile. I figure safest place for the prisoner is in Marcelino's jail until morning. Things will have cooled down a little by then, I hope."

"Maybe," Halvers said in a doubtful voice. "The woman's family, the Brackens, and some of their friends are hatchin' up something. I been watchin' them. We'll sure hear from them sometime. Probably tonight."

"No doubt," the marshal replied. "Take a look out in the street, Carl. See what's happening out there now."

The deputy moved out, going down the hallway to the courtroom. In a few moments he was back.

"Crowd's thinned out a mite. Most of them have drifted down to Sandalman's place. Big bunch out in front of the hotel, too."

"Cal ought to be back soon," Baca said, thinking of the other deputy.

The steady scratching of Conley's pen was loud in the room. Abraham studied the sloped shoulders of the clerk for a moment. Then, "Which way you taking him to Capital City, Tom?"

"Up the old Diamondback Trail," Kilgore answered. He pulled a thin, misshapen stogie from his pocket and thrust it between his lips. "Figure that will be the safest way to go."

The judge nodded his approval. "Good idea. Everybody will be expecting you to take the main road."

"How many deputies will you be taking?" Baca wanted to know.

"One," said Kilgore. "Halvers, here, will do fine."

Abraham frowned. "Guess you know your business but are you sure that's enough protection?"

Kilgore chewed at his cigar. "Two or ten, doesn't make much difference. With just three of us I figure we can move faster and quieter if we have to. Besides, a big bunch of deputies would sort of prove the law is still on the weak side, wouldn't it?"

Abraham considered that for a moment. "Yes, guess you're right. But don't take any chances. You know what your orders are if things go wrong."

Kilgore nodded. He swung around to Baca. "Where the hell's that deputy, Marcelino?"

Baca walked to the door at once. "I'll find out," he said. He opened the paneling. The deputy was there, just in the act of knocking. Before the sheriff could ask his question, he spoke.

"Got a wood hauler stopped back of the building, Sheriff. His wagon's loaded. We could walk alongside it to the jail without attracting much notice."

Baca said, "Good." He turned to Kilgore. "You ready, Marshal?"

Kilgore said, "Let's go," then paused. "Everybody here understands there's to be no talk about us taking the Diamondback, I reckon. I don't want that to get out."

They all murmured their assent. "How about you, Conley?" the lawman called to the clerk.

Conley, writing busily, looked up. "Of course, Marshal. Wasn't paying you no mind, anyway."

"Good." Kilgore reached for Coe's arm. "All right, Duret. Let's get out of here while we got a chance. Might not get a second one."

CHAPTER
SIX

C. J. Preston, the banker, stood near the front of the courtroom idly fingering the heavy gold watch chain draped across his paunch. He stared thoughtfully at the door through which Marcelino Baca had hustled Turk Duret to safety. Behind him Kilgore and a couple of deputies were moving the crowd into the street, clearing the building. He had come to the trial prepared to testify as to his losses at the hands of the outlaw but Duret's unexpected admission of guilt made it unnecessary.

He turned then and moved slowly towards the exit, nodding to Kilgore and the deputies, their chore completed, as they walked by him. He came out onto the gallery fronting the building and stopped. Directly ahead of him were the Brackens and several of their friends. Two men were assisting the stunned Todd to walk. In that moment C. J. Preston wished his only desire was to see Turk Duret dead! Todd Bracken was lucky. How would he feel if he had lost thirty thousand dollars, a loss destined to mean not only bankruptcy but disgrace and arrest for fraud as well? Fraud — that was a polite word for it. Those people who had trusted him would call it plain thievery!

36

But how could he have anticipated such a thing as a bank robbery?

Had not Duret raided the bank everything would have worked out well in time. The large losses he had incurred in that New Orleans stock venture would have been covered in a few more months. Now it was too late. As soon as the lawyers and examiners checked the records, the whole thing would be out in the open. And the men in Chicago who had backed him would not be satisfied with so small a thing as an apology and explanation. Hard cash was the only thing they understood.

Preston trembled. There must be a way out of it somehow!

Duret had done the job alone. He had been captured before he had time to spend even a dollar of the thirty thousand; therefore, it was reasonable to believe the entire amount lay hidden still, placed there by Turk Duret when he realized his capture was imminent. But where?

The cave where he had holed up with the Bracken woman and child had been thoroughly searched. Under his own, personal supervision every square foot had been dug into and carefully examined. And the area around the cave's opening as well. Nothing.

The marshal had been unable to get anything out of the prisoner either. Kilgore had questioned him at length shortly after his arrest and while Preston had not been given an opportunity for talking to Duret, he knew the lawman had tried his best to learn the whereabouts of the stolen money. The outlaw simply refused to talk.

But there must be a way to force him — there had to be! A man just couldn't allow his entire life to be thrown away by another's refusal to speak.

He let his gaze run the hot, dusty street. There was a sizeable knot of people gathered in front of Sandalman's Saloon listening to a harangue by some individual Preston could not distinctly see. Further along, near the hotel, he saw the Bracken family again. His eyes came to a halt halfway between. Tibo Waggoner and Bill Ford. The two men were slouched against a hitch rail looking on. They were strangers to Salvation but Preston had become acquainted with them and their unsavory reputations while he was below the border checking into some mining property a year or so past. Both were the sort who would do anything for a price. Preston's eyes began to light up as an idea came into his mind. He removed his hat and nervously scrubbed at the sweat on his balding head.

Why not?

He hurled the question at the last vestiges of conscience clamoring within him. *Why not?* He could be no worse off — and if handled properly, the plan would work. He could find out from Conley when Kilgore planned to leave with Duret and the way they would go. A few gold eagles would loosen the clerk's tongue. Waggoner and the men he would need would come higher but they would get the job done.

They were the sort he must deal with now. *My own kind*, he thought with bitter revulsion, remembering his own secret crimes. Yet, that was the way it had to be. A desperate man takes desperate measures. He came off the porch and started down the street. He must see Waggoner and talk it over with him. But he would have to be careful. It would not do to be seen talking with the gunmen.

Laurie Bracken and her father were close on the heels of Orville Stelder and Pete Brookerson, who were helping her brother along the street. Todd was groggy from the treatment he had received in the fight with Turk Duret and was having difficulty in keeping his knees stiff. But now that they were outside, away from the withering heat in the courtroom, he was recovering quickly.

"This sure ain't over yet," she heard her father say. He was looking at the jail, his eyes bright and hard.

Orville Stelder moved up to stand beside her. The Stelder place was a scant five miles south of the Brackens'. For the past year Orville had been paying court to Laurie.

"You're sure right, Mr. Bracken," he said. "Ain't nobody going to do something like that to our womenfolk. Comes night, we'll take that Duret out of that there jail and string him up higher'n a buzzard's roost."

Pete Brookerson came into the conversation. "You believe what the judge said, about them going to really hang him in Capital City?"

"Naw," Orville answered. "That's just another way to keep him alive until they find the money. That's the way

39

these here politickers work. Horse tradin' all the time. I bet that's all Preston's doings."

Laurie glanced at her brother. "You all right now, Todd?"

"I'm all right," he said gruffly. He turned to Stelder. "We got enough men lined up to break Duret out tonight?"

"More'n enough," Stelder replied. "Just ready and waiting for the word. That bank clerk had some friends. And there's the cowboys who was working for that rancher, all just honin' to get their licks in. Then, I figure we can count on some of the local citizens who don't like the judge's sentence."

"Any plans made?"

"All we've got to do is pass the word. Name the time and place."

"Front of the jail, soon as it's full dark," Todd said.

Laurie shuddered at the grimness of her brother's words. He was like a stranger to her since the death of Molly and the child. Once they had been a happy family. Hard working and poor, like most all the settlers in the valley. Turk Duret had changed that. He had cast a blight upon their lives and now, seemingly, they existed for only one thing — vengeance. A tremor again passed through her slender body.

"Todd," she said, laying her hand upon his arm, "do you think it's the right thing to do? Wouldn't it be better to let the law handle it? The judge said he would be hanged. I don't see how they can keep from doing it now. And with all those deputies around, there's going to be shooting. And more killing."

"Not much," Orville scoffed. "Them deputies are all for show. I don't figure they're going to hurt anybody protectin' Turk Duret. They just got to make it look good."

"Won't be no difference, anyhow," Saul Bracken observed. "He's going to be strung up, one way or another. Man's been sentenced. Us hanging him will be just as legal as the Territory doing it."

"And it sure won't make no difference to Duret," Stelder added with a laugh. "Either way, he's a dead one."

Laurie shook her head. "I still think it is the wrong thing to do," she said in a weary voice. "It can only mean more trouble for us. And more killing."

Harvey Conley waited until the lawman and Turk Duret had departed before he spoke.

He said, "I'll have these papers ready in a couple of minutes, Judge, if you want to sign them. Like to get them to the marshal this afternoon so's we'll be done with the case."

Abraham settled heavily into his chair. He mopped at his florid face. "This case won't be done with until they cut Duret down from the scaffold. You know that."

"Yes, sir," the clerk replied, nettled by the jurist's sharp tone.

Abraham adjusted his spectacles and read the document slowly. "Damned if your penmanship doesn't look more like chicken scratches every day, Harvey!" he muttered. "Where's the pen?"

Biting back his anger, Conley supplied the necessary item. Abraham laboriously wrote his bold signature across the bottom of the sheet.

"No pleasure," the judge said then, rising. "Sending a man to his death never is. Even a killer like Turk Duret. What do you reckon made him do a thing like killing Molly Bracken and her baby, Harvey? What gets into a man's blood and turns him into a monster?"

"Sure don't know," the clerk replied, stacking the sheets of paper together. "Money, most likely. Thirty thousand dollars is a lot of money."

"I suppose," Abraham murmured, staring at the floor. "Other men have done much more for less. For thirty pieces of silver, in fact."

The clerk nodded his agreement. "You think the marshal will have trouble getting him to Capital City? That's a long ride and people sure are steamed up about it."

"All he can do is try. I don't figure he'll run into any trouble he can't handle. Tom Kilgore is one of the best."

"Wouldn't surprise me none if a mob don't try to take Duret away from the law tonight."

"I'm of the same opinion. So are Kilgore and Baca. That's why they swore in a half a dozen more deputies. But I think they can take care of things the rest of this day and tonight. By morning the crowd will have cooled off and most of them forgotten what it was all about."

"And nobody's going to figure the marshal will be riding the old trail."

"Now, keep that under your hat!" Abraham warned sharply. "We don't want it known they're taking that road."

"I won't say anything!" Conley replied quickly in an injured tone. He reached for his hat and placed it on his small head. "Guess I'll trot these papers over to the marshal."

"All right," Abraham said. "Mind your tongue now!"

Anger flooded through Harvey Conley again. A hasty retort sprang to his lips but he clamped his thin lips shut and held it back. He would be a fool to flare up now; it would spoil everything. Best to just sit tight until he was ready to make his move.

He walked out onto the gallery and halted. The street was still crowded. People stood about in small and larger clusters all along its length. *Trouble for Kilgore and Marcelino Baca*, he thought. Movement at the corner of Engleman's Bakery, just opposite, caught his attention. He squinted his near-sighted eyes at the figure standing there. It was Mr. Preston. The banker motioned for him to cross over.

"Now what you reckon he wants with me?" Harvey Conley wondered aloud, starting across the street.

CHAPTER
SEVEN

At last the day's wilting heat was beginning to break. Inside the cramped jail quarters Kilgore, Baca and two of the deputies, along with their prisoners, had waited out the painful, dragging hours. On the front gallery three more special officers had maintained a shotgun vigil over the milling crowd. Kilgore rose and moved to the door. Opening it a few inches he briefly surveyed the street. When he came about, his square face was serious.

"Not thinning out much. Thought the heat would break up that bunch some, but looks like I guessed wrong. Appears to me there's about as many out there now as there was this morning."

"It's the Brackens that's keeping them stirred up," Carl Halvers stated. "Got their minds set on swingin' their own hang noose."

"Keep that to yourself," Kilgore snapped. "We've got enough trouble without you dropping that idea into somebody else's head."

The blond deputy shrugged. He shifted his glance to the stagecoach bandit, snoring softly on his cot. "All this ruckus sure ain't botherin' that jasper any. Bet he's mighty glad he ain't the one they're after."

"He would if he'd sober up long enough to think about it," the other deputy observed dryly.

A yell went up in the street. Kilgore immediately moved again to the door and peered out. He said something to the deputies outside and then, stepping back, closed the thick panel and dropped the bar into place, securing it.

"What happened?" Marcelino Baca asked.

"Some fool with a rope," Kilgore answered. He stood for a long minute in the center of the room, a huge, square-shaped man, staring with unseeing eyes at a calendar on the back wall. Suddenly bringing his attention to Baca, he said, "When they bringing us some grub, Sheriff?"

"Six o'clock."

"Near that now. Maybe you ought to see what's holding it up. Might not get a chance to eat after it grows dark."

Baca got up at once and moved to the rear door, Kilgore trailing after him.

"Tell Homer to bring plenty of coffee," Halvers called after them.

Kilgore followed the sheriff out into the dusk. He said something to him, glanced about the narrow alley behind the jail building and returned.

"He hear me?" Halvers inquired.

"Hear you what?"

"Tell Homer to bring lots of coffee."

"He heard you," Kilgore assured him.

He slowly walked the breadth of the small room. The dead heat trapped within its walls was like a smothering blanket and sweat stood out on the big lawman's forehead in beansized beads. He halted before one of the small, barred windows. It was open but it admitted only a meager amount of air.

"Around dark," he said, thinking aloud. "That's when they'll make their play."

"You plan to stop them, with guns, I mean?" Halvers questioned, picking up the thread of the lawman's thoughts.

Kilgore nodded. "If we have to. My job is to get Duret to Capital City. Alive. I intend to do just that."

The deputy wagged his head. "Don't make much sense. Maybe kill some of the town's citizens to keep Duret alive so they can hang him later."

"It's not a question of Duret's life," Kilgore said, patiently. "It's a question of which is stronger, the law or a lynch mob. If we're to have law and order in this Territory, it will begin right here tonight in this town of Salvation. We keep Duret alive so the Territory can hang him, it means law has been established. If that mob out there takes him away from us and lynches him, then we're still an outlaw frontier."

"Maybe so," Halvers continued in that doubting way of his, "but if some of those people out there get hurt tonight, there'll be the devil to pay. They'll take this jail apart, piece by piece. And us along with it."

Kilgore cocked his head, looked sideways at the deputy. "You thinking about turning in your badge now, in case that happens?"

"Not me!" Halvers exclaimed, his face reddening quickly. "Just saying what's liable to happen, that's all."

46

Something thudded against the front of the building; a rock, most likely, thrown by someone in the crowd. Yells lifted and there was an outburst of gunshots. Immediately afterwards there came a soft knock at the back door. Kilgore moved to open it, covered by the guns of both Halvers and the other deputy. It was Baca, a tray in one hand. Behind him was the waitress from the Bumblebee Cafe, bringing a second.

"Inside. Quick," Kilgore said, stepping back to admit them. "Anybody see you come this way?"

Baca set his tray on the desk and motioned for the girl to do likewise. "Don't think so, Tom. We came through the hotel."

"Somebody's going to finally remember about that alley," Kilgore said, pulling the cloth off the trays. "And when they do, we got our hands full. You go back the same way you came, miss," he added to the girl. "Don't want anybody seeing you leave here."

The waitress was staring at the man she took to be Turk Duret, her eyes filled with a bright interest and fascination. "Yes, sir," she murmured, easing slowly for the exit.

"Let her out, Carl," Baca directed.

Kilgore took one of the plates, heaped with beans, fried potatoes and meat, and pushed it under the grating to Ben Coe. "Better eat all this. You'll be needing it."

Baca thrust a second plate into the cell of the other prisoner but the man did not arouse. The sheriff left it and turned to the desk where the other lawmen were beginning to eat.

"How about Chrisman and the other boys?" Halvers wanted to know, motioning to the deputies standing guard in front of the building.

"We'll spell them soon as we're finished," Kilgore replied. He poured himself a second cup of coffee.

The glass in the street-side window suddenly shattered. A shower of sharp particles spread across the floor. Halvers, startled, leaped to his feet. His plate overturned, spilling its contents. Kilgore threw a quick glance at Baca.

The sheriff shrugged. "I guess this is it."

Kilgore got to his feet. He swung to Halvers. "Get outside with the others, Carl. It's dark now and they'll be needing some help."

The deputy immediately picked up his shotgun and moved to the door. Kilgore opened it. His appearance was met with a burst of yells and questions. The marshal hesitated a moment and then followed Halvers onto the porch.

Lifting both hands for silence, he said, "You people go on about your business. You're wasting your time around here."

"You think so, Marshal?" a voice challenged from the crowd. "We're giving you a chance right now to turn Duret over to us. The last one we'll give you. You don't take it, we're coming in after him."

Kilgore shook his head. "Nobody's coming in after anybody. Try it and there will be somebody that gets hurt. These deputies have orders to shoot and shoot to kill if they have to."

"We can do a little shootin', too, Marshal," another voice replied. "Don't be forgettin' that!"

"Then you will all be guilty of murder and I'll see to it that every man jack of you stands trial on that charge! Now, get away from here. Go home. Go on down to Sandalman's and get yourselves drunk. I don't want any trouble with you."

"You got it, anyway, Marshal," a man's deep-throated voice stated. "Plenty more than you can handle."

Kilgore heard the solid thud. He saw Carl Halvers spin half about and drop his shotgun. Blood streamed down the front of his face. A rock, about the size of a man's fist, clattered up against the wall of the jail.

"Keep an eye on that bunch!" Kilgore yelled to the remaining deputies. "Shoot only if you have to."

Taking the luckless Halvers under the armpits, he dragged him back into the building. A clamor had lifted in the street at sight of Halvers' falling and the lawman knew that time was suddenly running out. The mob had tasted blood and, like the witless animal it was, would press its advantage now.

"Wrap something about Carl's head," Kilgore said to Baca. "Have to stop the bleeding ourselves. Can't risk getting a doctor yet."

He wheeled about to the cell where Ben Coe sat. "Come on, we're getting out of here."

The sheriff looked up in surprise. "You going to start now? What about a deputy?"

"Have to try without one," the marshal replied. "Better you have a full force here. Give us as long as you can but don't let things go to gunplay before you open up and let them see we've gone."

Baca signified his understanding. In a low voice he said, "Then it's my move."

"Then it's your move, Marcelino," Kilgore said quietly. "Good luck."

"The same, *amigo. Vaya con Dios.*"

Kilgore stepped to the rear door, Ben Coe close at his heels. The marshal opened the panel and checked the alley.

"Empty," he said with satisfaction. "Where will those horses be, Sheriff?"

"Fifty yards to your right."

Kilgore and Ben Coe stepped outside, into the darkness and turned down the narrow corridor. They found the horses, three of them, saddled and waiting as Baca had said. The two men mounted up and, once in the saddle, Kilgore lifted his hand for silence. There was a steady rumble of talk broken by sudden yells, back at the jail. The sounds were growing louder, more insistent. The crowd would not be stalled much longer.

"Let's get out of here," Kilgore said. "Straight down the alley until we hit the end of town. Then we'll take the main road."

Coe lifted his manacled wrists. "How about taking these off?"

In the darkness Kilgore grinned. "Not the handiest things a man can wear, are they? Reckon we better wait. No time to spare now."

Wheeling his horse around, he started down the alley. Ben Coe was not far behind.

★   ★   ★

Todd Bracken was standing near the north edge of the pulsing, swaying mob gathered before the jail. At that moment the door had just slammed, shutting off his view of the unconscious Carl Halvers. The jam of yelling, cursing people was moving in closer. Somewhere a voice was shouting for a log, a ram of some sort with which to batter down the door. More rocks were being hurled and another deputy was struck but the stone only grazed his shoulder.

"No place here for you," Todd said then, turning to Laurie. "Things are going to get bad in a few minutes. Go on down to the hotel and wait for us there."

The girl shook her head. "I'm staying right here," she said stubbornly. "I want to be around in case you or Papa get hurt."

"But you shouldn't —"

"Shouldn't see a man lynched? Why not? Other women in this crowd will. Why shouldn't I?"

"Not so much that, Laurie. You might get hurt. Even shot."

"The deputies won't do any shooting," she said, quoting words she had heard earlier. "That's what you all were saying this morning."

Todd Bracken started to make a reply, paused. His eyes had picked up two riders, far down the street. They had emerged from a passageway next to Canady's store. Both looked familiar. He felt his sister's fingers close about his wrist as she too, saw the riders.

"Todd! That's the marshal — with Turk Duret!"

51

A shaft of lamplight from Canady's fell across the pair at that moment. It glittered briefly upon the star worn by the lawman, glinted sharply off the chains that linked the prisoner's hands.

"It sure is," Todd murmured. "They're sneaking Duret out of town."

He laid his finger against Laurie's lips, pressing her to silence. Better if they said nothing about it. They could handle it themselves with their own group. He reached for his father and pulled him to his side.

"Just saw Kilgore ride out with Duret. We're going after them."

Saul Bracken's reply was an angry yelp. "Dang that blasted marshal! We ought —"

"Hold it!" Todd snapped. "We don't want the whole town knowing about it. Let them stay here and throw rocks at the jail. We'll take Pete and Orville and do this on our own."

"Don't count me out," Laurie said firmly.

Todd glanced at her, frowning. He saw there was no use and little time to argue. "All right. Now, Pa, you and Laurie go to the wagon yard and get us some horses. I'll hunt up Pete and Orville."

"There's Pete now," Saul Bracken said.

Brookerson shoved his way towards them and halted. Todd quickly explained what had happened, what he planned to do.

Brookerson nodded. "Good. We can handle it better alone, anyway. My horse is over in front of the saloon.

52

I'll follow up the marshal and Duret so's we don't miss them. You catch up soon as you can."

"We won't be far behind you," Todd said. "Just be damn sure you don't lose them!"

CHAPTER
EIGHT

Kilgore and Coe reached the end of the alley and halted.

"This way," the marshal said, after a moment, and swung his horse up a narrow passageway lying between two false-fronted buildings.

They reached the street and once again paused. Several hundred yards to the right they could see the restless mass of the crowd before the jail. Except for that, Salvation appeared to be deserted. More rock throwing was in progress at that moment and, while they watched, a half-dozen men supporting a railroad tie between them, trotted into the street. A chorus of yells greeted them immediately and the crowd parted to receive them.

"Time to get out of here," Kilgore said. He touched the horse with his spurs and rode into the open, passing through a shaft of light lying across the roadway by the lamps in Canady's windows. Coe followed and they moved out at a brisk trot for the first mile. After that distance, Kilgore pulled down to a walk.

"Turnoff is just ahead," he said to Ben. "We take the right and swing towards the mountains." Digging into his pocket, he produced a key. Handing it to Coe, he said, "Better get those cuffs off. You'll be needing both hands once we're on the trail."

Coe removed the manacles, stuffed them into his saddlebags. "Keep them handy, in case we run into company," he said. "Think we've fooled that mob?" he added.

"For a spell, anyway. All we need is a little head start. And a couple of days. Big job for us is to keep anybody interested in Turk Duret, dogging our tracks. That will let Baca get Duret to Capital City."

"Two days' ride, somebody said," Coe answered. "Shouldn't be too tough. You got my gun?"

"Long two days," Kilgore said and handed the deputy his weapon.

They rode on through the night, bearing due east in the direction of the rugged-rimmed Los Pinos Mountains.

"That fool lawyer!" Kilgore suddenly exclaimed. "Allison, or whatever his name was. Thought for a minute there this morning that big mouth of his was going to get us all lynched."

Coe grinned. "Hope that's the last time I'm called on to play outlaw. That crowd really had blood in its eye!"

"Little close, all right," Kilgore commented.

"Sort of funny, going to all this trouble just so Duret can hang in Capital City."

"More to it than that, than what Abraham said back there in the courtroom. This Territory wants statehood in the worst way. Before it can get it, it has to prove it's ready. Got to show those Eastern senators and bigwigs that it's come out of the frontier class and has established good law and order. Trying Duret and executing him through due process of law will be a mighty strong argument in our favor."

"So that's it. Figured there was more to it than just some whim of the governor's. He know about your plan to get Duret there?"

"No. We just told him we'd have the man there for the execution. Didn't go into any details. You don't take chances on a leak in a case like this."

In the velvet blackness of the night Ben Coe scratched thoughtfully at the scar on his neck. The horses moved steadily on, covering the soft ground easily. The only sounds were the rhythmic creak of saddle leather, the breathing of the animals. Stars were out, shedding their faint, silver light. The moon was only a vagrant shadow, slipping in and out of the clouds.

"That Bracken family," Ben said then, "you know them before this all happened?"

Kilgore said, "Nope. First time I ever saw them was here in town, why?"

"The daughter, the sister of Todd Bracken, she's the one I helped that night I rode in."

"Real pretty girl," Kilgore said. "Good thing she didn't get a look at you —" The marshal's voice broke off suddenly. He twisted half about in the saddle and listened. "You hear something behind us?"

Coe cocked his head to one side. "Not just now. Thought I heard a horse back there somewhere, mile or so ago."

Kilgore settled and relaxed. "What it sounded like to me. Hardly seems possible anybody could have got on our trail this quick."

"Unless they saw us ride out and followed."

In that next instant both men heard the telltale sound; the unmistakable click of a shod hoof against rock.

"Somebody sure back there," Kilgore said in a low voice. "Let's lose them."

He spurred his horse into a full gallop and Ben Coe followed his example. They rode hard and fast for the next hour, keeping to the trail that circled the towering hills. They were gradually climbing and after a time, they were compelled to pull up and allow the blowing horses to rest.

"Road we want is on the other side of the mountain," the marshal explained. "When we reach it, we cut back to the north. Diamondback Trail, they call it. Runs along parallel to the valley road the stagecoach uses except the mountains lie in between. Once we get on the Diamondback, I figure we're in good shape."

They were back in the saddle in a quarter hour but the going had become steeper and traveling was much slower. Eventually they reached a crest, however, a low-running hogback, topped out, and descended to the shallow canyon on the far side. At the forks where one road bore directly on eastward toward the flat, Texas plains, they took the other, striking northward on a fairly level trail.

They kept the horses at a good pace for the better part of an hour, hoping to reach the more heavily timbered areas before halting for sleep and rest. Neither man had spoken for miles, being intent upon their purpose but finally, as a dark band of trees drew nearer, Kilgore reined in beside Coe.

"We'll make camp in that grove. Horses can't keep going at this rate much further."

Coe nodded his agreement. He could use a bit of rest himself. He glanced ahead. The grove the marshal had indicated was a small one, a dark, triangular patch spewing out onto the low hills from the higher mountains to the left. He could smell the clean, fresh odor of pine as they drew closer.

Quite suddenly four men stood before them. A fifth, still mounted, waited off to one side in the shadows of the trees. Starshine glinted brightly off the rifles and pistols held by the men.

"Far as you go, Marshal," one of the four said, his voice vaguely familiar. "You and Duret just climb down off them horses. And keep your hands where we can see them."

CHAPTER
NINE

Ben Coe sat quietly on the buckskin, hands half lifted, and waited out the moments. From the corner of his eye he could see Kilgore, also with his arms up.

"What's this all about, Bracken?"

The lawman's voice was cool as spring rain. The four men facing them moved out into the open. One Coe recognized as Todd Bracken, the slain woman's husband, who had jumped him in the courtroom. The old man was his father. The other two were strangers to him, either close friends or relatives of some sort. He shifted his gaze to the fifth member of the ambush, the one yet mounted. With a start he saw it was Laurie. In the darkness of the grove she sat very still and straight on her horse, her face a pale oval in the meager light.

"Git yourself down off them horses!" old man Bracken commanded again. He waved the long-barreled rifle in his hands. "We don't want no trouble with you, marshal. We just aim to carry out the judge's sentence and string this here killer up ourselves."

"That's a job for the Territory, Bracken," Kilgore replied without moving. "And it will be done if you'll keep out of it. Only thing this will get you is a lot of grief."

"Can't see how," one of the strangers drawled. "Court said to hang Duret. That's what we figure to do. We'll just be savin' the Territory all that trouble."

"You hang him," the marshal stated in clipped words, "and you'll face a murder charge!"

"Now, you tell me what the difference is," the rider persisted, "if we do it or the Territory does it? Either way the judge's orders will be carried out."

"Ain't no use arguing with him, Orville," Todd Bracken said, speaking for the first time. "That's all that's been going on all day — just talk." He stepped nearer Kilgore and Ben Coe. "You getting off those horses or do we drag you off?"

Kilgore shuttered a glance at Coe. The marshal shrugged and nodded.

"Keep them hands up!" Saul Bracken yelled in sudden alarm. "Like I said, we don't want to hurt you none, Marshal, but you try somethin' and you're a dead man. Ain't nobody goin' to keep us from hangin' Turk Duret!"

In that hot, tense moment Ben Coe swung slowly down from his horse. He could feel the pressures building up within him and he began to understand more clearly the dangers that faced him. It was one thing to confront death for your own sake — entirely different when you were doing it in another man's place. And he was helpless to do anything about it!

Kilgore could not talk, nor could he. To reveal to the Brackens now that he was not the genuine Turk Duret but a decoy to draw off any who sought to capture him,

60

would upset the whole, carefully planned ruse. And they would be off at once to intercept Marcelino Baca and the real Duret almost before the sheriff and his prisoner were out of Salvation.

"Get the marshal's iron, Pete," Saul Bracken said. "Why, look there, all of you!" he added, his voice rising. "He ain't even got Duret tied up! No ropes or nothin' on his hands. You sure are trustin', Marshal."

Kilgore made no answer. He stood motionless while Pete cautiously drew the pistol from its holster and thrust it into his own waistband.

"Where's that rope?" Todd Bracken asked, his voice grim.

Old man Bracken turned to the girl. "Laurie, fetch us that rope."

The girl dismounted and came forward. She handed the coil to her father and returned to the shadows where she had been waiting.

"All right, Duret, come on. You too, Marshal. Both of you walk up ahead. We got a good tree all picked out."

"Laurie!" Saul Bracken called again. "Lead that buckskin over here. Reckon a man ought to go a-settin' his own horse."

Kilgore had not moved. He stared at the four men lined up before him. "I'm warning you for the last time, Bracken. You do this and I'll see you all hang for it!"

"Maybe so," Todd Bracken replied, stepping forward. "But I don't reckon there's a jury in the country that

61

would convict us for what we're doing. Duret murdered my wife and baby. I got a right to see that he pays for it."

"Eye for a eye, tooth for a tooth," old man Bracken sang out.

"But you've got to let the law handle —"

"We ain't got much faith in the law," the man called Orville broke in. "We figure, before they'd hang Duret, they'd make themselves a deal with him so's they could find Preston's money."

"That's damn fool thinking!" Kilgore retorted angrily. "Everything the judge told you this morning was pure truth. Duret will hang just as soon as I can get him to Capital City. You can take my word for it."

There was a long, uncertain moment of silence, a hush laden with the promise of sudden violence. Ben glanced at Laurie. She wore a pair of faded Levi's and a shapeless old shirt, evidently one cast off by Todd. He wondered how she felt about the matter.

"Let's get on with it," Todd Bracken said quietly. "I can believe you, Marshal, but I can't trust those people in Capital City."

Ben caught the signal from Tom Kilgore. As one they lunged forward, straight into the four men. A gun exploded in Coe's face, blinding him momentarily. He felt the hot blast of the muzzle, heard the scream of the bullet as it sped by him. Todd was directly before him and he struck out. Bracken dodged and the blow skated harmlessly off his shoulder. Ben felt something, a rifle butt likely, come down across his back. The force was light and it merely staggered him.

Saul Bracken was yelling at the top of his voice, "Don't shoot him! Save him for a hangin'!"

Coe heard Kilgore gasp as the wind was driven from his lungs. He flung a glance at the lawman. He was down on one knee. The man named Pete was swinging at his head with a pistol butt, a second blow, apparently. In that moment Coe felt a pair of powerful arms clamp about his legs. Orville was rushing at him, fists swinging. He tried to duck away but Todd Bracken had him anchored to the spot. Orville's hamlike fists crashed into him, one high on the chest, the other just grazing his chin.

He lashed out at Todd, trying to break the man's viselike hold on his legs. His hand connected with Bracken's skull and did no damage. Orville was pounding at him again, striking at his face. Ben dodged and fought back, feeling his fists drive into yielding flesh. But he was having little effect, he knew; trapped as he was by Todd Bracken, he could get no leverage and no power into his swing.

He cast another look at Kilgore. The marshal was trying to get to his feet. Saul Bracken was swarming in on him, rifle held, clublike, overhead. Ben yelled a warning. In the same instant Orville's balled fist found its mark. Coe felt the shock of it behind his ear, felt it streak through him and set up a sort of paralysis. His arms at once were heavy and there was no strength left in his trembling legs. Orville's grinning face began to blur.

Vaguely, he heard a gunshot shatter the night. It sounded hollow and distant but the flash was nearby. There were horses. And more men.

A voice called out, "Hold up there! What's going on?"

CHAPTER
TEN

Coe was out only brief seconds. Even as he crumpled to earth his brain began to clear. On hands and knees he shook his head savagely, throwing off the filmy webs shrouding his mind.

"Stand away from them!"

Faintly through the haze Ben heard the sharp command. It was followed immediately by Saul Bracken's protesting reply.

"This ain't none of your business, sergeant. Just you and your soljer boys keep right on goin'."

"Maybe it is army business," the sergeant answered. He rode up close to Coe and the still prone Kilgore. "This the marshal and the man he's taking to be hung?"

The lawman groaned and stirred. The soldiers and the others remained silent while he struggled to a sitting position. He rubbed at the back of his head. Blood streaked down from one corner of his mouth and there was a raw, ugly scratch crossing the left side of his face. Brookerson and old man Bracken had used him plenty rough.

"You the marshal?"

Tom Kilgore lifted his glance to the sergeant. "I am," he said, studying the man. He was a husky, broad-faced individual who sat his McClellan like a partially emptied sack of grain.

"Then I reckon you're who we're lookin' for." He swung down from his horse. He threw a glance at the soldiers who remained mounted. "Keep your rifles on them people. They try something, shoot."

Kilgore had gotten to his feet, as had Coe. The sergeant faced the marshal. "Mighty glad we found you and your prisoner. Didn't have much idea where you'd be."

Kilgore grinned. "I'm glad, too. A few more minutes like we were having and you and your boys would have happened by too late."

The soldier nodded curtly and backed toward his horse. "You all right?" he asked of Coe as he moved by.

Ben shrugged. He rubbed at his jaw. "I'll get by," he said.

The sergeant nodded and climbed back into the saddle. He swung his attention to the Bracken party.

"Now, you people mount up and get out of here. Be quick about it. I don't want any trouble with you!"

Todd Bracken took a quick, angry step. "Keep out of this, soldier! No call for you to butt in!"

"Got my orders," the sergeant replied coolly.

Orville Stelder laid his hand on Todd's shoulder. He shook his head. "No use trying to fight the army. Reckon we'll have to let the Territory hang Duret."

"No, by God!" Todd yelled and lunged at Coe. "That's for me to do! They're not cheating me out of it!"

The crack of the sergeant's pistol shattered the long quiet of the grove. From nearby a startled bird whirred blindly off into the night. The bullet threw up an explosion of trash and dust at the feet of Todd Bracken. He halted.

"Next time I won't be aiming at the ground," the soldier said coldly. "Next time that bullet will go plowing into your belly."

The three remaining soldiers, at the crack of the gun, had ridden forward and now ranged out alongside their burly leader.

Laurie, too, had reacted. She uttered a low scream and ran to her brother. She threw her arms about him and held him back. But Todd Bracken made no further attempts to reach Ben Coe. He stood, spread-legged, hands hanging at his sides while a white hot hatred burned in his eyes.

"No cause to hurt anybody, sergeant," Tom Kilgore reproved mildly. "Just give these folks a chance and they'll be on their way. They're kin to the dead woman. Can't blame them much for how they're feeling right now."

"Best thing they can do is get out of here," the soldier observed sourly. "I won't take no back talk from people such as them. They want trouble, me and the boys can sure accommodate them."

One of the soldiers laughed. Kilgore glanced at him. And then back to the sergeant. He frowned. "Didn't get your name, sergeant," he said and moved nearer.

"Waggoner. Tibo Waggoner. Men with me are Bill Ford there. And George Kemm. Third one is Chancey Desmond."

The lawman nodded to each. He turned his back to them, faced the Bracken party. "I'd suggest you move out right away. Wouldn't want to see any of you hurt."

Saul Bracken grumbled his agreement and they all started for their horses, tethered just within the grove. Coe and the others watched them depart moments later. They rode westward, up one of the many long canyons that apparently would lead them to the ridge and down the opposite slope.

When they were beyond sight and sound, Tom Kilgore rubbed thoughtfully at his bruised chin. "A close one. Sure glad you happened by, sergeant."

Coe saw Kilgore pause and deliberately await the soldier's answer, as if much depended upon it.

"What I was told to do, Marshal."

"So? Told to do what?"

"Meet you and the prisoner and ride escort to Capital City."

Kilgore continued to stroke his jaw. "That right! Real thoughtful of them. Who gave the order?"

"Came straight from the Governor. Seems he's right anxious for you and your prisoner to get there safe."

In the semidarkness Kilgore's face betrayed none of the suspicion Coe knew was clouding the lawman's mind. The marshal ducked his head, as if he understood and came slowly about.

"Don't think it is safe to camp here rest of the night. Never know what those Bracken people might take in mind to do." He swung his eyes to Ben Coe. "Mount up, Duret. We're moving out."

Ben knew what was passing through the marshal's thoughts; that the Governor knew nothing of their plan to reach Capital City, that he had no idea of when they were even starting, in fact. It all added up to one thing. Sergeant Tibo Waggoner and his men, despite their cavalry uniforms' were fakes.

Ben saw Kilgore heave his bulk onto the saddle and rein about. He watched the lawman's face for some indication of the next move, of his plans and what was expected of him. But the darkness made it difficult to see any signal from Kilgore. Remembering then, he dropped his hand to the right saddlebag, lifted its flap and prepared to snatch up the gun hidden there.

"Let's go," the lawman said, looking at Coe straight on.

Ben kneed his horse around and Kilgore fell in beside, almost knee to knee. Waggoner and his three riders dropped into the double file a few feet to the rear. They followed the wagon track trail, barely visible by starlight, through the dense stand of pines.

"Be ready to move out fast," Kilgore murmured, leaning forward to adjust his stirrup. "I give the word — break out for the trees. Keep going north. We'll meet up later."

Coe said, "Right."

"Don't know what these jaspers have got up their sleeves but I don't figure it's good. Thing that bothers me is how did they know we were taking this trail?"

"The Brackens knew."

Kilgore muttered. He straightened up. "Reckon that's so. But they could have seen us leave and followed. Maybe taking a shortcut they knew to head us off. But Waggoner and his bunch came in from the north — like they'd been waiting along the road for us. Sure would like to have the answer to this."

"You figure they're some of Duret's gang?"

The lawman shrugged. "Could be. One thing I'm sure, they're not soldiers and the Governor didn't send them."

"Don't see how they could be any of Duret's outfit, unless they had never seen Duret. They would have spotted me at once."

"Was just thinking that. Could be somebody hired them out to do this job."

They rode steadily on, getting deeper into the higher mountains. The chill of the greater altitude began to make itself felt, a welcome change from the day's driving heat. Waggoner trotted his horse up beside Kilgore, his heavy face dark and shadowy in the pale starshine.

"How much farther you plannin' to go, Marshal?"

Kilgore shook his head. "Another hour maybe. You boys getting tired?"

Waggoner said, "Can't see much use ridin' all the night. Might as well camp around here somewheres."

"Good place about ten miles on. We'll stop there."

Waggoner made his grumbling reply and dropped back to his original position. Kilgore waited until he was beyond hearing distance.

"We reach the foot of that slope ahead, there's a sharp bend to the left. Trees are thick on both sides of the road. We'll make a break there. You go left and I'll go right. Good luck."

Coe nodded and said, "See you up the line," and set his gaze on the slowly approaching turn in the road. When it was only yards away he risked a casual glance over his shoulder, determining the location of the men behind them. Waggoner and his bogus soldiers were a scant thirty feet away. Getting quickly beyond reach of their guns was going to be a hard chore. But there was no other answer.

The slope reached ground level, dissolving into the plains and revealed a bulking knob of rock jutting upward. Ben could see the thick stand of pines flowing out to the right and assumed a similar grove lay to the left. At that moment it was hidden from his view.

"Make the turn," Kilgore said softly, "then go for it."

Coe tensed in his saddle. He drew abreast of the rocky bulge and set himself for a sudden plunge, off into the protective blackness of the pines. Together he and Kilgore made the sharp curve.

"Now!" Kilgore yelled and drove spurs into his horse's flanks.

Both mounts leaped forward, Ben only slightly behind the marshal. Coe swung hard left and drove hard for the nearest cover, only a dozen yards distant. Tom Kilgore was whirling off to the right for a similar haven.

Waggoner's hoarse yell lifted behind them. A gunshot blasted through the night. Ben clawed at his saddlebag, reaching for his own gun and found nothing. It was gone, apparently taken by the Brackens earlier. Another shot flatted through the darkness, echoing along the canyons. He heard the whine of the bullet and involuntarily ducked. A half-dozen more shots rapped out after that, some coming from Kilgore. There was a pounding of hooves off to the left; Waggoner's men closing in, trying to cut him off. If he could have another few seconds, he would make it, he would be inside the trees.

That was when he saw Tom Kilgore.

The lawman's horse was curving back toward the road at an uneven trot, seemingly uncertain where to go. Kilgore was doubled over the saddle, arms dangling loosely around the animal's neck. The thought, *he's hit*, flashed through Coe. Immediately he swerved from his course and rode for the marshal's side. If he could grab the reins, there might still be a chance they could reach safety.

The shooting had ceased when he changed his direction. He raced across the open ground and snatched up the trailing leathers and thundered on towards the shelter of trees. Suddenly he was aware of riders all about him, rushing in. Ducking low, he pressed the buckskin for more speed.

"Hold it, Duret!"

Waggoner's harsh command rapped at him from only inches away, it seemed.

"Pull up, unless you want the same as the marshal got!"

CHAPTER
ELEVEN

Ben Coe hauled the buckskin back on its haunches. Around him, in a swiftly closing noose, Tibo Waggoner's men swept in.

"See if he's dead, George," Waggoner snapped at the man nearest Kilgore.

Kemm sidled over to the lawman and grasped him by the shoulder. He pulled backwards. Kilgore's body slid brokenly to the ground.

"Sure looks like it," Kemm commented, staring down at the marshal. Kilgore appeared to be no more than a pile of dusty clothing.

"Make damn sure!" Waggoner directed, in the same tone. "Don't want no loose ends draggin'."

Ben watched the rider dismount, a deep and bitter anger eating through him. Hell of a way for a good man like Tom Kilgore to die — shot in the back by a bunch of hard case outlaws. He deserved better.

"He's dead," Kemm announced. "Two bullets got him. Both in the chest. One in the heart, I reckon."

"Drag him over there into the brush where he won't be seen, case somebody comes along," Waggoner said. "Bill, catch up this horse of his. Don't want him wanderin' back to town. Might set folks to askin' questions and lookin'."

Keeping a tight rein on his anger, Ben Coe asked: "You not going to bury him? Ought to. At least put him in a grave."

Tibo Waggoner swung to Coe. "No time for that, Duret. What difference it make to you anyway? He ain't nothin' but a John Law. For a man who took a woman and kid into the hills and let them croak, you're mighty soft-hearted all of a sudden!"

Coe settled back into his saddle, acutely aware in that moment of his responsibilities, of the part he must play. He was Turk Duret to Tibo Waggoner and anyone else until Marcelino Baca had delivered the real killer to Capital City. So much depended upon it; and already Tom Kilgore's life had been sacrificed for it. He would have to watch himself. The idea of the marshal's body being callously dumped into the brush had infuriated him to such a point he had almost tipped his hand!

He shrugged, pulled his mouth down into a hard grin. "Makes no difference to me," he said. "Man just hates to think about the coyotes and buzzards getting to a body — any body."

Waggoner laughed. "Reckon it won't make no difference to the marshal. He ain't feelin' no pain where he is."

The two men who had dragged Kilgore's heavy figure off the road returned to their horses. Ben made a mental note of the location, determined inwardly he would return and give his friend a proper burial. That would be after Baca had delivered his prisoner and after he saw to it personally that Waggoner and his crew were under lock and key for the murder of the lawman. But first came the matter of staying alive, of coming back.

He swung his glance to Waggoner, knowing the hatred he felt for the outlaw glowed through his eyes. "What's next? What's this all about, anyway?"

"You'll find out quick enough," Waggoner replied. "Me and the boys and a friend of ours have got a little business with you."

"Meaning what?"

"Meanin' just what it sounds like. Now, suppose you head right on out the way we was goin'. And don't try no tricks. We'll be watchin' you like a horny toad watchin' a bluebottle fly and the first thing you do will mean a bullet where it hurts. We don't aim to kill you 'cause we got to keep you alive but they ain't nothin' says we can't make you feel mighty miserable."

Ben urged the buckskin into motion up the trail. He slowly sorted the bits of information he had gleaned, trying to fit them into a picture. "Who's this friend you're talking about?"

Waggoner laughed again, the sound harsh and unpleasant in the night's stillness. "You'll find out, bucko. Just keep ridin'. Your friend Kilgore didn't know it but he was headin' right where we wanted him to."

Coe considered that. "You mean to Capital City?"

"Nope. Got a little shack up here in the hills. Real quiet sort of place. Figure we won't be bothered there while we ask you a few questions."

"Questions?" Coe prodded.

Waggoner grinned, his broad teeth gleaming whitely in the half light. "Questions like where you stashed that money you hauled out of Preston's bank. We figure we'll get the answer."

Realization struck Ben Coe at once. Believing him to be Turk Duret they planned to force him into telling where he had hidden the thirty thousand dollars the outlaw was reputed to have stolen. And they would employ any and every method to loosen his tongue. Men like Tibo Waggoner stopped at nothing! Well, he would just have to stand and take it. If Tom Kilgore could give his life for the cause, he could do his part by keeping his mouth shut, at least until he was certain Marcelino Baca had delivered his prisoner.

How long would that be?

Two days — three at the most, Kilgore had said. That promised to be a long time. Ben Coe asked himself the important question — could he stand it? Could he manage to hold onto his senses, keep his mouth closed under the punishment Waggoner and his men would dish out to him? A man could only try, he assured himself; could set his nerves and his will and try.

Another thought came to him then as he rode wearily along: escape. For one thing he did not like the idea of traveling northward; if Waggoner and his mysterious partner discovered somehow he was not the genuine Turk Duret they would suspect a ruse and immediately rush to lay an ambush outside of Capital City, hoping to make an interception there. The farther north they were, the quicker they could reach such a point.

If he could manage an escape, he might be able to lead Waggoner and his bunch off onto a different direction, to the south perhaps and thus gain some advantage. That Waggoner would not dare kill him was evident now; dead he could not reveal his supposed secret as to where Preston's money had been hidden.

He glanced back over his shoulders, first the right and then the left. He was well attended, being in the center of a crescent formed by the four men. Tibo Waggoner saw his move and trotted up closer.

"Gettin' ideas, Turk? Don't. You wouldn't make ten feet before you caught a half-dozen slugs in your back."

"Little hard to make a dead man talk," Coe said dryly.

Waggoner only shrugged and returned to his position. Coe looked ahead. They were well into the mountains now. The brush along the trail had thinned out to more sturdy junipers and pinon trees. Beyond them were pines with the thick, triangular silhouette of a spruce making an occasional appearance. To the left he saw the ghostly, white flank of a sandstone escarpment denoting they were climbing well towards the summit of the range. To his right a narrow wedge of blackness laid its shape. At sight of that Ben Coe's hopes lifted. It would be a narrow, probably deep canyon running at right angles to the road and most likely well overgrown with brush. A man might dodge quickly into its depth . . .

Back upon the ridge a coyote broke the steady *clop-clop* of the horses' hooves with his lonely, fragile wail. Almost immediately his reply, coming from somewhere farther along the escarpment, echoed forlornly.

"Dang them critters!" one of the riders swore softly. "Ever' time I hear one, I get the creeps."

"Just you be glad they're real coyotes and not a pack of Apaches gettin' ready to jump us," Waggoner replied. "Ain't been so long ago, they might have been."

"You right sure they ain't now?"

"Been no Indian trouble 'round here for two, three years."

"Can always start again. Hear old Victorio and his bunch ain't so happy on the reservation."

"They'll stay there," another of the riders said and then added with a laugh, "us soldiers'll see they do."

"Sure will be glad to get out of this suit and on a real saddle again! Can't figure how them cavalry boys sets one of these things all day. Like ridin' a pack rig."

Ben listened idly and watched the wedge of blackness draw closer. Purposely he slanted his horse in a gradual line for the right side of the road. That six feet could mean the difference between success and failure if his chance came; between life and death, to be more honest. He glanced to the sky, soft, velvet-like black with the stars swung just out of arm's reach. A good overcast would have been a welcome advantage but the heavens were clear.

"What you figurin' to do with your share of the money when we gets it?"

78

Ben listened to the rider's question. *Keep talking, keep talking, get your mind on something besides me,* he thought. His gaze was fastened on the canyon, now less than a dozen yards; thirty feet — twenty. Coe kept his eyes riveted to the edge of the arroyo. If it was too deep he would have to forsake the idea. No use breaking the buckskin's legs in a hopeless attempt, not to mention his own neck. Or if the floor was loose rock instead of sand, it would be a bad risk.

Ten feet.

Ben Coe tensed in the saddle. He shortened the reins, gathering them in his left hand while he patted the buckskin's neck reassuringly. He strained his eyes to see exactly what the wash offered. It was narrow at that moment and not very deep. Four or five feet, he judged, dropping swiftly as it sliced away. It appeared to be mostly filled with brush which was good.

"Maybe we ought to talk to —" one of them was saying.

Ben drove spurs into the buckskin. He doubled forward over the saddle and yelled, as they sailed off the edge of the wash. His cry was a wild, discordant, echoing sound that split the night. But it had the desired effect; he was already plunging into the brush before Waggoner and his men had recovered from their confusion.

CHAPTER
TWELVE

The buckskin landed on all fours, went to his knees on impact, recovered. A half-dozen shots rang out and bullets clipped through the brush with a vicious, whirring efficiency.

"Don't shoot him, damn it!" he heard Waggoner shout. "Get him alive!"

Coe headed the plunging buckskin down the arroyo, thankful for the smooth, sandy bottom. But brush was there, thick and hindering. It slashed at him, clawed at his clothing and dragged at the horse. A gnarled juniper curving over the wash almost knocked him from the saddle. They were bearing eastward, slightly north. He threw a desperate glance ahead, hoping the arroyo would double back, swing to the south. But deep in the cleavage he could tell very little about its course.

Waggoner and his men were close behind him. The crashing their horses set up in the brush informed him of their nearness. The advantage was his, at least for the moment as he had a few yards lead and the brush effectively screened him in the darkness. And they would not shoot, he knew that now.

"Get him! Get him!"

Waggoner's strident bellow echoed above the racket of the horses. The rough going began to tell on the buckskin. His sides were heaving and his willingness to leap the brushy barriers was less eager. But their mounts also would be tiring and if the buckskin could not maintain the pace, neither could the horses pursuing.

"Couple of you — head him off! Get out on the bank and circle ahead!"

Waggoner's command instantly set up its worry in Ben Coe's mind. They could easily do just that, climb out of the arroyo to the level ground bordering either side. A horse could stretch out there and soon overtake and pass anyone down in the impeding brush. Coe threw a hasty glance to his left and to the opposite side. Tibo Waggoner's men were too close for him to try a similar plan; he had no choice but to keep on, following the floor of the wash — and hope for a break.

The buckskin had given about all he had. He started to falter, to stumble. A branch caught at the bridle and he shied, off balance. The stiff limb sprang free and struck Coe sharply across the chest and he grabbed the horn to keep from falling. Another stand of briar barred their way. He reined the buckskin to one side, avoiding it, going partly up the bank of the wash. The husky little horse fought gamely to keep his feet, stumbled, regained his stride and came into a small clearing beyond the thorn patch. Two of Waggoner's riders, the ones he had sent to circle ahead, were waiting. The buckskin skidded to a stop.

All the pent-up hatred engendered for Waggoner and his men by the murder of Tom Kilgore; all the personal anger and frustration built up within Ben Coe during the past moments suddenly fused within the man and burst. He left his saddle in a low, flat dive straight at the two men sitting side by side both on their horses.

He struck them with animal fury. His powerful arms reached out for them, looped over their shoulders, dragged them both to the ground amid the churning hooves of their horses. Both men yelled in surprise and fright. Heedless of his own danger, Coe lashed out at the nearest, felt the satisfying yield of flesh under his knotted fist. He struck again, missing and staggered as one of them caught him from behind.

Waggoner and the other men were there by then, piling off their horses and coming into the fray. Ben saw a face loom in close and drove it to the ground with a straight right. He felt hands claw at him, settle about his arms. He went to his knees, was dragged back up. Fury still raging through him he struggled to break free, to drive his fists again and again into these enemies. A hard jolt to the side of the head rocked him. Another into the belly sent the wind gushing through his lips. His head swam and lights danced before his eyes.

"Get a rope!" Waggoner's voice ripped through the haze. "Just so you'll know we ain't foolin' around with you no longer, Duret!"

Coe's breath was coming in painful gasps. He tried again to break free but strong hands pinned his arms to his sides. Fingers dug into his hair, jerked his head back.

"Wind that rope around him and set him on his saddle," Waggoner ordered. "I'll take no more from this jasper tonight."

Coe vaguely felt the rope bite into his arms, cinching them against his ribs. He was half carried, half propelled to the buckskin and hoisted aboard. As his senses slowly cleared and his breathing dropped back to normal, he heard the outlaw's voice again.

"Chancey, hang onto that buckskin's reins and don't lose 'em. He gets away again I'll bend a gun barrel over your head!"

Ben glanced at the man who reached for the leathers. He was dabbing at his nose which was bleeding freely. He had been one of those who had blocked the way in the clearing. Coe grinned at the man.

"You won't be laughin', come mornin'," Desmond said sourly and led the buckskin back to the trail.

"Climb out of this wash," Waggoner said when they were all mounted and together. "Too hard travelin' and we already lost time."

Coe steadied himself as best he could in the saddle while his horse followed the lead rider up the embankment onto level ground. His attempted escape had not profited him much, an hour possibly two at the most. But two hours would put Marcelino Baca that much nearer Capital City. It had been worth it.

They cut straight across the flats until they once again were on the main road. There they swung northward, keeping at a steady pace that was not too hard on the horses and that carried them deeper into the mountains. Towards the morning they were beyond view of the mesa, with hills completely surrounding them. At a shallow canyon they turned off and climbed sharply for a quarter mile through dense pines to break, finally, into a broad clearing. Daylight was just beyond the ridge to the east when they pulled to a stop before a low-roofed cabin.

"Here's home, Mister Duret," Tibo Waggoner said sardonically, waving his hand at the poor structure.

Ben let his eyes drift over the place. Two horses, still saddled, stood at the hitch rail on the south side. A faint wisp of blue smoke trickled from the chimney. The door of the cabin swung back, setting up an overloud creak in the early morning quiet. Two men walked out onto the sagging gallery. One Coe recognized instantly — the slight, stooped shape of Harvey Conley, Abraham's clerk. The second was an older man, much larger, with balding head and a round belly that overlapped his belt.

"Here you are, Mr. Preston," Waggoner said, "just like you ordered."

C. J. Preston, the banker.

CHAPTER
THIRTEEN

Here was the answer — Conley had been the only other person to know they planned to ride the Diamondback Trail. Coe was thankful, in that moment, the jurist and the lawman had withheld their trust at that point, that Conley had not been taken into their confidence as to the real and the bogus Turk Duret. And Conley, somehow, was hooked up with Preston.

Preston walked closer, his small mouth pursed, his eyes hard glinting. He looked Coe over carefully and then swung his attention to Waggoner.

"You were a long time getting here. Have some trouble?"

"Some," Waggoner admitted. "He tried to make a break for it. Had to run him down."

"Kilgore?"

"Dead."

A frown pulled at Preston's features. "Bad, plenty bad. Couldn't you have avoided that? Don't like the idea of having a federal man's death on our hands."

"Better get used to it," Waggoner said dryly. He swung down from his saddle. "Take these horses around to the rail, Chancey."

The others dismounted and Waggoner stepped up to Coe to assist him.

Conley said, "Well, guess my job's done, Mr. Preston. You give me my money and I'll be moving on."

Preston glanced at the clerk. "Not yet, Harvey. We still have to find out where Duret hid it."

"But that wasn't our agreement!" Conley protested mildly. "You said all I had to do was tell you when Duret and the marshal were leaving town. And the road they were taking. I've done that."

Preston shrugged. "Can't pay you until I get my hands on that money. I'm broke."

Conley's thin shoulders sagged. "What am I going to do? I was figuring on pulling right out for California. Now I got to wait. And I can't go back to town."

"This won't take long," Waggoner said, pushing Ben towards the shack. "I got a feeling Mister Duret will talk pretty quick."

Ben staggered across the porch and into the shadowy, squat room. It was a single square, four walls, dirt floor and a ceiling through which light was beginning to leak. A broken table canted in one corner with two upturned nail kegs beside it for chairs. The only other furniture was a small, sheet-iron stove, weakly alive against the morning chill.

"Set down," Waggoner directed, shouldering Coe to one of the kegs. "Be smart now, Duret, and we'll get this over with in a hurry."

"I'll handle this, Tibo," Preston said in a low firm voice.

86

"Then get at it," Waggoner said, stepping away. "I'm about done in, ridin' all night. And we ain't got much time to waste."

"Shouldn't take long," Preston said smoothly, sitting down on the other keg. "Duret's smart enough to realize his best bet is to talk. Now, why don't you and the boys scrape together a little breakfast for us? Supplies there in that sack."

Ben knew what was coming, what lay ahead for him. First the easy approach, the velvet glove tactics by the banker. Then, if that failed to produce the desired results, Waggoner's way of handling things would be used. He had a moment's wonder about Marcelino Baca; where would he be at that daylight hour? Well on his way to Capital City undoubtedly, but not far enough along yet. Coe braced himself. It was his job to delay Preston and Waggoner to the limit of his ability and strength.

He glanced at the banker. "Don't know what you got in mind," he drawled, "but I'm not talking about anything until you take these ropes off me. Hardly breathe."

"Take them off," Preston ordered. Waggoner and George Kemm stepped up and released the knots.

"There'll be a gun on you every minute," Tibo Waggoner said. "Try and run for it and we'll shoot your legs out from under you."

"He won't try," Preston said. "He knows better."

With the binding pressure of his bonds gone, Ben felt better. The numbness began to fade as unrestricted circulation worked through his body and it was easier to take a full breath. Nor did he feel so utterly helpless.

"Maybe we ought to get him a soft blanket now," Waggoner said sarcastically. "Could be his tail end is a mite tired from settin'."

Preston ignored the remark. "Duret, I'll come straight to the point. We got you loose from the marshal for one reason — the money you stole from me. I want it back. Where did you hide it?"

Ben gave the man a hard grin. He shook his head. "Something you'll never know, Preston."

From out of nowhere, it seemed, Waggoner's open hand came arching downward and crashed into the side of Coe's head. It knocked him off the nail keg and into the wall. For a minute Ben lay there, shaken to his heels, caught against the rough logs. Slowly, he regathered his scattered senses. After a time he managed a grin.

"Get you nowhere," he said to the glowering Tibo. "Might as well save yourself the work."

Waggoner drew back his arm for a second blow. Preston shook his head. "Don't be a jackass, Tibo. Knock him senseless and he certainly won't be able to talk. There are plenty of other ways."

Full daylight now lay across the ridges and peaks and streaked through the openings in the cabin. George Kemm moved to the outside and hunkered near the fire over which Desmond and Bill Ford were frying salt pork and boiling coffee.

"Save yourself a lot of pain, talking now," Preston said then to Ben. "You see what Tibo's like."

Coe shook his head.

Waggoner swore loudly in disgust. "Still think the only thing this jasper will understand is a damn good workin' over. Give me ten minutes with him and I'll sure guarantee he'll be ready to talk."

"Or never talk again," Preston said acidly. "No, we can always try that. Let's have a bite to eat and give Duret a chance to think things over."

He arose and walked to the doorway, Waggoner's hulking shape at his heels. At the opening, both men halted.

"Duret won't be eating, Chancey," the banker said in a voice meant to reach Coe. "We'll just save his plate for him until after he's talked."

The smell of the bubbling coffee filled the small room, as did the frying meat and potatoes, but Coe was not particularly hungry.

"Mighty fine stuff," Bill Ford called, lifting his cup in a sort of salute.

Ben changed his thoughts to other matters, to the necessity for keeping his wits about him; to the death of Tom Kilgore, to the Brackens. Had that family forgotten their desire for vengeance and returned to Salvation? He thought of Laurie and the memory of her filled his mind. He hoped she had not shared the feelings her hate-crazed brother and father indulged themselves with. When this job was over with, he would return to Salvation and find her. He would explain what had transpired, make his position and true identity clear. She would understand, he was certain.

"Come on, come on," Waggoner's grumbling voice came through the doorway, breaking into Coe's thoughts. "Let's get this over with."

"What's the hurry?" Preston asked. "You said Kilgore was dead so he can't give us any trouble. Nobody knows where we are and there's not enough time gone for them to miss Duret yet. We got today and tomorrow, if we need them."

"I ought to be leaving now," Harvey Conley said in a faint voice. "Don't think it's a good idea for me to be hanging around."

"Maybe we ain't got as much time as you figure," Waggoner said, poking at the fire.

Preston glanced sharply at the outlaw. "What does that mean? Something you never told me?"

"There's the family of the woman Duret killed. The Brackens. We jumped them when they was about to string Duret up. We run them off but it could be they're still hangin' around somewheres."

Preston studied the cup of black coffee in his hand. "Well, that's possible, but I doubt it. Might be they'd go back to town and one of them would say something about soldiers running them off. But I doubt if they will do any talking at all. Otherwise, they might have to explain what they were doing with Duret and the marshal in the first place."

He finished his drink and set the empty cup on a flat rock near the fire. Rising, he motioned to Waggoner and started for the door of the cabin. They entered and Ben watched Preston take his place on the nail keg.

"You've had time to think things over, Duret. You ready to talk now?"

Coe looked straight into the eyes of the big man. "What would I gain by telling you anything?"

"Only that you'll be dead by sundown if you don't."

"Be dead anyway, once I reach Capital City. Die one way or another, it's all the same."

"Little foolish hiding all that money so nobody will ever get any use from it. Be a sad waste."

"Anyway, you had yourself a big time with that woman," Waggoner put in. "Reckon that was better than money to a man who'd been cooped up alone for a long spell."

Ben lifted his gaze to the heavy face of Tibo Waggoner. The man was actually enjoying the thought. Holding back the angry words that sprang to his lips, he said, "Far as I'm concerned, nothing is better than money. You ought to know that."

Preston nodded his understanding. "My own sentiments exactly. Maybe we could work up a deal, Turk."

"What kind of a deal?"

Waggoner growled his disapproval. Preston ignored the man. "Lot of money involved. Suppose we split —"

"No, by God!" Waggoner exploded and struck at Coe. "We don't split with nobody!"

Ben ducked the wild swing. He came swiftly to his feet and drove a straight right into Waggoner's face. It stopped the outlaw cold. Ben turned him around with a left that cracked when it landed, doubled him over with a right to the belly. Preston yelled and backed to the opposite wall. Coe tried to snatch the pistol from Waggoner's holster. His fingers brushed the butt of the weapon but Tibo was coming to and twisting away. At that moment Kemm and Bill Ford rushed into the room, summoned by the noise.

They crowded in upon him. Coe went over backwards, off balance under their combined weight. He came up against the table and it collapsed under him. Fists lashed out, striking him in the body, on the face, on the head. His breath was suddenly gone, driven from his lungs by the crushing weight of the two outlaws, bearing him down. He felt a stinging blow, heavier than the others, and realized someone was kicking him. The sharp point of a boot drove into his ribs and the small of his back time after time. He tried to squirm away. Something smashed against his chin and he felt no more.

He came back to his senses dripping water. He was lying on the floor, atop the shattered table. Tibo Waggoner stood over him, an evil, vicious grin on his broad face as he poured the contents of a bucket onto Coe's head. Ben gasped, sucking deep for breath.

"Feel like a little talk now, Mister Duret?" Waggoner's voice cut through the fog.

Ben shook his head, faintly aware of the outlaw's arcing boot immediately lashing out at him. He tried again to roll away. The blow missed his ribs, caught him just behind the ear. Blackness once more engulfed him.

Some intuitive, subconscious caution kept him still when he revived the second time. He opened his eyes to mere slits, making no movements with his body.

92

Preston and Waggoner stood near the doorway. The sun was two-thirds up the morning sky and the thought reached Ben Coe that he had gained a few more precious hours by his actions. If he could hold out a while longer — at least until sundown! He heard a step, saw Preston and Waggoner move back to allow George Kemm, carrying a bucket of water, to enter.

"Pour it all on him," Waggoner ordered.

"Don't you be so damned quick to lay a hand on him this time," Preston snapped. "Give him a chance to talk."

"You ain't havin' much luck your way," Waggoner replied sourly. "Goin' to take somethin' besides jawin'."

Water cascaded down upon Ben, still feigning unconsciousness. Maybe he was a fool to take this sort of punishment but he would hold out and do his part. Somehow.

CHAPTER
FOURTEEN

That day, wearing slowly from morning into afternoon, was a succeeding nightmare of blackness and light. A lesser man would have never survived, but Ben Coe's grim determination and animal stamina carried him through. Toward evening, however, he knew he could not last much longer. Eventually he would break, not of his own volition, perhaps, but involuntarily under the stress of pain the truth would be out.

Near sundown he stared with glazed eyes through the open doorway. Preston and Waggoner, close to exhaustion themselves from frustration and their own violent efforts to loosen his tongue, were conversing in low voices. Beyond them he could see George Kemm and the other outlaws, Desmond and Ford. They had removed the uniforms they had been wearing and were dressed now in the customary range clothing. He could not see Harvey Conley anywhere and had a moment's wonder about that.

He lay there, body throbbing, eyes burning with a fever-like intensity. His ears and the bones in his head ached. Where Waggoner's descending boot had struck his jaw, a loosened tooth beat a steady cadence of pain. But he had survived the day and that was some reward;

Marcelino Baca would be well out on the valley route with his prisoner by that time. Yet, he was not in the clear. There still was no good margin for absolute safety. Hard riding horsemen could circle the mountain and cut him off. More time was needed.

Coe began to cast about in his fogged mind for an idea, a plan that would keep Preston and the outlaws occupied for another day. Or, at least until noon of that next day.

"How about it, Bill?" Waggoner called to Ford. "Ready yet?"

The outlaw walked to the fire. Bending over he took up the long handle of an axe, the metal part of which had been nestled in the glowing coals. "Ready," he answered.

Waggoner laughed harshly. "Reckon Mister Duret will do some talking now! A red hot axe blade on his naked belly will make him do most anything!"

Ben Coe knew instantly this was the end of it. Such pain would turn him into a babbling madman in a few short moments. No matter how hard he fought to keep his lips sealed, the story would come out. From the depths of desperation a plan suddenly evolved; one that might gain him the night and most of the next day. It could cost him his life but he was beyond the point of caring much about that. He thought the plan through to a conclusion and decided it was worth a try.

He struggled to a sitting position. "Preston!" he called.

The banker and Tibo Waggoner heard and wheeled instantly. They came quickly into the cabin.

"Ready to talk, Turk?"

Ben nodded. "Had enough," he said thickly through bruised lips.

"Told you I knew how to open him up," Waggoner chortled. "Should have let me work him over sooner. Saved us all this time."

Preston paid the man no attention. "Glad to hear it, Duret. Hate treating a man like we've had to treat you."

"You said something about a deal," Coe began, feeling a little stronger.

"No deals!" Waggoner cut in roughly. "We don't need to make none with him now. He'll talk, anyway."

"Maybe," Ben replied. "But like I said, dying here in this shack won't be any worse than dying on the end of a rope in Capital City. Maybe easier, in fact. Now, if you want anything from me, you'll listen."

"We'll listen," Preston said. "Rest of you keep out of this and let him say what he's got on his mind. Go ahead, Turk."

Behind the pair Ben could see the other outlaws standing just outside the doorway. Harvey Conley was there, too, his narrow face drawn and anxious.

"Here's my offer," Ben said. "I want five thousand dollars of the money and a horse to get to Mexico on."

There was a long, strained minute of quiet. Tibo Waggoner suddenly laughed. "That what you want? Why, sure, we'll go for that, won't we, Preston?"

Ben saw Waggoner cast a wink at the men outside. His chances for winning in such a deal, were he really intending to try it, would be about as good as bringing Tom Kilgore back to life. He stared at Waggoner. "I

96

want Preston to say it. He seems to be running this outfit."

"I agree," the banker answered quickly. "Five thousand and a horse. The one you were riding. And we'll go you one better, Turk. We'll see that you get to Mexico without any trouble."

Coe said, "Good. We've got a deal."

"Now," Waggoner said, rubbing his palms together, "where's that money stashed?"

Ben glanced at the big man and laughed. "Tell you now and have you sneak out of here tonight and grab it for yourself? Not much, Tibo. I'll take you to it tomorrow."

"What's wrong with goin' there right now?"

"Plenty," Ben said, flatly. "Long ride, for one thing and, thanks to you, I've got to have some rest. Way I feel, I couldn't make fifty yards. And I need some grub."

"Hell with that —" Waggoner began angrily but Preston silenced him.

"Morning will do all right. We all could use some sleep. Once we get the money, we'll have a hard ride ahead of us so we better be ready." He turned to Ben. "Place where you hid the thirty thousand, it close by?"

Ben shook his head, thinking fast. "Like I said, it's a long ride. South of here. Back towards the town."

Waggoner thought that over for a minute. "Somewhere around that cave, that it?"

Coe said, "Pretty near. Have to see the place to find it." The plan was working well. And most important of all, they would be riding south, in the opposite

97

direction to Capital City. He would be leading them away from Marcelino Baca and his prisoner.

"You able to walk?" Preston asked then. "Come on outside and eat. Plenty of food and coffee left. Then we can bed down for the night."

Ben got stiffly to his feet. His head spun from the effort and he staggered drunkenly when he walked but he managed to make it to the fire. George Kemm handed him a plate of meat and potatoes and a chunk of hard tack. Chancey Desmond poured him a cup of the black, steaming coffee. He sat down on the ground and ate hungrily while the others looked on.

By the time he had finished, the sun had dropped behind the ridge to the west and night was coming on. The outlaws had removed their blanket rolls from their saddles and were spreading them near the fire. Ben stood up and started for his buckskin, intending to get his own woolen and canvas.

"Never mind," Waggoner said quickly. "I'll fix you a bed."

Taking the roll, he paused for a time and glanced about the camp. Spotting a sturdy, young pine some thirty feet or so from the fire, he walked to it. Kicking aside several branches and rocks lying beneath it, he spread Coe's bed.

"Over here's where you'll sleep," he called to Ben. "Bill," he added, "bring me some rope."

Ben moved to the blanket and sat down. Ford, a coil of rope in his hands, and followed by Preston, came up.

"Just want to be sure Mister Duret's comfortable — and will be here when we wake up in the mornin'," Waggoner said, taking the rope from Ford.

He cut off a short length and handed it back to the cowboy. "Tie his hands. Behind his back, now. And be damned sure he can't get loose. I'll just use the rest of this to hobble him and picket him to this here tree."

In a few minutes they were finished. Ben, lying on his side, knew there was no chance at all of escape.

Preston smiled down at him. "Sorry about this, Turk, but we can't take any chance on you changing your mind. Just be for tonight. After tomorrow you'll be on your own again."

Ben nodded. Tomorrow would bring other problems. But he was too tired to think about them now. He watched Preston and the two outlaws walk back toward the fire. He was asleep before they reached it.

CHAPTER
FIFTEEN

In that cold hour preceding dawn, Ben Coe came suddenly awake. He was stiff and sore and his body was a single, continuous ache. He lay completely still and let his swollen, half closed eyes study the outlaw camp. Something had roused him from his slumber. It had been none of the men near the fire for, with the exception of George Kemm who was crouched over the small flame soaking up some of its heat, they were yet asleep.

He remained unmoving, senses gradually becoming more acute as the moments wore on. Lying, as he was, on his side, he could see all of the men. Preston was near the cabin. Waggoner and Bill Ford on the far side of the fire. Chancey Desmond and the clerk, Conley, a few feet to their right. In the pale light they were barely distinct but he could make out their features. He shifted his gaze to the peaks in the east. The first flare of daybreak was shooting its long fingers into the sky.

"Don't move!"

The words were a hoarse whisper, coming from behind him. Hope sprang alive within Ben Coe. He felt a tug at the rope binding his wrists. Cold metal touched his arms, rubbed slowly back and forth against them for a few moments and then his hands were free.

"Don't move!" the warning came again. "Stay like you are."

He was aware of fingers working at the bonds that pinned his ankles together. And they, too, were released. Coe lay quietly, waiting.

"You got one chance," the whisper advised him. "While they're asleep, crawl back into the brush that's behind you. You'll find a horse about fifty feet away."

The words renewed Coe's sagging strength, drove the pain and weariness from his body. Help had come; he had not dared hope for any but somehow it had arrived. He tried to place the voice but could not.

"When you get the horse, follow me. I'll be waiting."

Ben heard the slight rustle of brush as the man returned to the skirting thicket along the clearing's edge. He tried to flex his muscles without making any outward movement. He must be careful. One wrong move now, one overloud sound and this chance for escape would be gone. And if he did manage to reach the cover of the bushes, could he run to where the horse had been tethered? His body was so cramped and stiff he doubted if he could walk, much less run any distance. But he would try.

He glanced to the camp, preparing to make his first move. Kemm still hunched over the fire but he no longer was the only man awake, Ben noted with sinking heart. Bill Ford was on his feet, stretching and yawning. Keeping his eyes squeezed to only slits, he saw the outlaw throw a look in his direction, then move around to Kemm's side. Taking up the soot-blackened coffeepot, he placed it over the flames.

Coe realized he must act quickly. In only moments, the rest of the men would be awake. And then it would be too late. He moved his legs experimentally, testing their strength and response. He would have to be as quiet as a cougar to get away from the tree and into the brush.

The throbbing of the many blows that hammered into his body faded as the time for action came. He tensed himself, planning each move, each foot of distance he must cover to the thicket. He would worm his way from the tree, keeping flat on the ground. When he reached the first stand of brush, he would rise. Then he would run, fast and quietly as possible. And it had to work the first time. There would be no second try.

He froze. Chancey Desmond had sat up. Ben remained motionless, keeping his body stiff and straight, as though the ropes still bound him. Desmond rubbed at his grizzled chin, scrubbed his cheeks. He said something to Kemm and lay back down.

It would be dangerous to delay any longer. They all would be awake in another minute or two. Ben began to work his way out of the clearing. The muscles in his legs complained at each move but he ignored the pain and crawled slowly on. His head throbbed with the straining effort and new aches slugged at his body but he gave no quarter and continued on.

He reached the first outcropping of taller growth and rolled into it, no longer keeping his eyes on the camp. He got to his feet, and with a fresh burst of pain shooting through him at the change, began to run. He kept low for another ten or fifteen feet and then came upright. They had not missed him yet! Now, if he could reach that horse . . .

He was moving at a long-legged, unsteady gait. It brought him full tilt against brush and trees alike. The impacts sent him reeling off but he drove on, heedlessly, jerking himself free of the clutching branches, stumbling over rocks and uncovered roots. He looked eagerly ahead, searching for the horse. It must be close now. Only fifty feet his rescuer had said. *Fifty feet.* It seemed like he had covered a mile already!

Back in the clearing a shout went up. They had discovered his escape. They would mount up instantly and give chase, knowing he could not have gone far on foot and was still in the nearby area. Ben tried to muster more speed but his trembling legs would not respond. His breath was coming in great, heaving gasps and his chest seemed to be filled with double-edged, sharp pointed knives. But he drove himself onward.

He saw the horse.

A broad beamed little white waiting patiently beside a gnarled and twisted juniper. The animal heard his noisy approach, shied to one side nervously. Coe attempted no soothing words. There was no time left for that. He simply had to chance it that the animal was securely tied.

He plunged into the small clearing, reaching for the reins looped into a slip knot. They came free at first jerk. One hand on the horn, one on the cantle, he dragged himself into the saddle, grateful the horse could shy no farther than the blocking juniper. Behind him he heard the crashing approach of Preston and his men, already beating through the brush for him. They were no more than moments off.

"This way!"

The same hoarse whisper reached him from the far side of the tree. Obediently he headed the white towards the sound, forcing him to break path through the brushy barrier. A short distance ahead, a rider on a buckskin was snaking his way expertly through the trees; a man, undistinguishable in the half light of the grove but somehow familiar.

Ben Coe asked himself no questions. It was enough that he had been delivered from the hands of Tibo Waggoner, Preston and the others. That their present pursuit of him was taking them farther away from Marcelino Baca was an added relief. He glanced over his shoulder, searching the forest for signs of Preston's men. He could see only the brush and the trees.

The man on the buckskin was leading him eastward. Ben kept the white on his trail, never allowing him to slacken his pace. A gunshot ripped through the quiet. A bullet clipped leaves overhead, thunked solidly into the trunk of a tree some yards past. They had spotted him.

He risked a hasty look. It was Bill Ford, again aiming. This time his bullet would likely find its mark in the white horse. The first shot had been a warning.

Ben turned to the man ahead. He was almost beyond view at that moment as he dropped onto a slight grade. They were entering a wide canyon, coming into it at right angles. Ben reached the lip and began his descent.

He watched the rider before him. The man was now swinging sharply back to the right, as a deer will do, to shake a pursuer.

In a few more moments they were reclimbing a gentle slope to a smooth running ridge. At once they dropped into the paralleling canyon, one of much greater depth. Faintly, off to the east, Coe could hear the shouts of Tibo Waggoner and the answers the others were making while they worked the rocky ground. It had been a clever move on the part of the buckskin's rider to double back on his own trail.

Ben glanced ahead. The crouched man was pulling his horse to a stop in the shadow of a pyramiding spruce. He urged the white toward him.

"I'm obliged —" Ben began, managing a smile through his swollen, battered lips.

The words died. The rider had whirled about in his saddle. A leveled gun was in his hand. Ben took a long breath, let it out slowly.

He had been following Todd Bracken.

CHAPTER
SIXTEEN

For the time of a dozen heartbeats the two men stared at one another. Bracken's face was taut, his mouth curved down into a bitter, hating arc. His eyes burned with an insane fire and Coe knew without second thought he was facing the final moments of his life. Todd Bracken, consumed with that driving need for vengeance, meant to kill him. There might have been a chance with Preston but not so with Todd. He could count on one thing — dying. Ben stirred in the saddle. Off to the east the sounds of Preston and his crew became fainter.

There was a rustling of the brush behind Coe, more subdued noises to the right. From the tail of his eye he saw Saul Bracken ride into the clearing. He was followed by the man they called Orville. And then Laurie. An odd feeling possessed Coe when she met his glance. It was something akin to thankfulness, relief. Or possibly it was something deeper. He gave her a wry grin and watched her lower her gaze before his. Somehow, his hopes lifted a little; something in her manner gave him the impression she was not as convinced he should die by their hands as were the others. And if that were true, he had at least one ally in the Bracken camp.

"You calculate you give old Preston the slip?" Saul Bracken asked, pulling up beside Ben.

Todd said, "Maybe for a spell. But he'll be back."

Old man Bracken grinned at Coe. "Like we was tellin' you, Duret, ain't nobody goin' to cheat us out of stringin' you up."

Ben glanced to the rising sun. A good six hours yet until noon. He rubbed thoughtfully at his neck. Still too soon to end the masquerade. Marcelino Baca and his prisoner should have those hours for safe margin. Somehow he must stall the Brackens — and continue to stall them. He turned to Todd.

"Don't know if I should be thanking you or not. Preston and his bunch were taking me back to where the money was hid. Then I was lighting out for Mexico."

"That's what we figured," Todd Bracken said. "But you're a fool if you think Preston would have turned you loose."

Coe shrugged. "He'd have no cause to kill me, once he got the money back. Anyway, a poor chance is better than no chance at all. And I don't even have that with you, I reckon."

"You're right," Todd Bracken said coldly.

Ben shifted his gaze to Laurie. She was studying him closely, the tan oval of her face serious. Coe shook his head.

"Still feel like it would be a mistake."

"Mistake? What would be a mistake? Hangin' you?" Saul Bracken's voice cracked with his impatience.

"No, just letting all that money lay there and go to waste."

There was a complete silence. Finally, the elder Bracken said, "You got some idea about it?"

"I could take you there. Rather see you folks have it than know it was going to stay there and rot."

"We're not caring anything about the money," Todd said, suddenly. "We don't want any of it!"

"Thirty thousand dollars," Saul Bracken murmured. "Sure is a lot of money. Does seem a shame, it just goin' to waste."

"Won't be doing me any good, if you folks are so set on stringing me up. Somebody might as well have it."

Orville Stelder said, "You feel that way about it, why didn't you tell Preston and his bunch where you hid it instead of takin' all that beatin' from them."

Ben rubbed at his neck again in that thoughtful way of his. "With Preston I had a chance, but with you folks, feelin' the way you do, why . . ." Ben shrugged.

"You goin' to tell us where you hid it?" Saul Bracken demanded, his voice lifting with eagerness.

"Well, like I said, somebody ought to have it." Coe paused, looked slowly about. He was taking up the minutes, allowing them to pass. "Any chance of my buying a ticket to Mexico if I do?"

"None," Todd Bracken snapped. "We don't want that money and couldn't keep it if we got it. You think you can buy us off for killing my wife and baby, you got another think coming!"

Ben, once again, allowed his gaze to switch from one of the party to another: Laurie, Orville, old man Bracken. "That the way you all feel?"

The girl made no reply. Orville tipped his head at Todd, indicating the decision was with him. Saul Bracken lifted his hands, let them fall.

"Up to my boy, I reckon."

"Forget it!" Todd snarled, suddenly angry and impatient. "Let's move out of here. Preston and his crowd will be doubling back this way and I don't want to run into them again."

"All right," his father grumbled. "Sure think we ought to talk about that there thirty thousand dollars a little more, howsomever. Ain't right, lettin' it go to waste."

They filed out of the clearing, riding southward. Old man Bracken led the way, followed by Laurie, Coe and Orville Stelder. Todd brought up the rear. Ben's eyes were on Laurie's slim figure directly ahead of him. Even in the shapeless, worn clothing of her brother, there was a full, sweet womanliness about her. He recalled, then, those moments earlier when he had caught her studying him. Was she trying to remember something? A man coming to her aid back along the trail just outside of Salvation, perhaps? He decided that could not be it. The night had been dark and he had taken care to keep his face concealed.

"Let's haul up and eat," Saul Bracken called back after an hour had passed. "Ain't put no vittles inside my belly since last night."

Todd murmured his assent. "Swing up the next draw you come to. Orville, you keep an eye on Duret. He tries to run for it, shoot him in the legs."

They rode up the narrow slash that turned off at right angles to the high hills and pulled to a halt beneath a broadly spreading cottonwood. The open space was small, confined and it was necessary to picket the horses a few yards distant in an adjacent clearing. Laurie at once began to prepare a meal, procuring hard biscuits, dried beef and some already boiled potatoes from her saddlebags.

"Watch that fire now," Todd warned as his father scratched up a small pyramid of dry twigs and leaves. "Don't want smoke showing for Preston to see."

Saul Bracken grunted. "Don't you be tellin' me how to pick ducks, boy! I was makin' fires with no smoke 'fore you was born."

Todd made no reply. He swung his glance to Ben Coe, the question he was asking himself apparent in his eyes.

Ben shook his head. "If you're wondering if you ought to tie me up, forget it. I'd be a fool to go chasing out there with Preston and Tibo Waggoner and all the rest beating the brush for me. Anyway, I still think you ought to listen to my proposition."

Todd said, "No, we're not listening to anything. We got one thing to do; get clear of Preston and then string you up to the nearest tree. You better start worrying about that."

Coe said nothing. He glanced to the sun. Now about two more hours until noon, he estimated. He cast

110

about in his mind for more ways to delay matters, to consume the dragging minutes. If he could only persuade the Brackens to take him to the cave where the money was supposedly buried! But Todd Bracken would not listen to such a proposal. He decided then to concentrate his efforts on old man Bracken.

"How far you reckon it is to that cave where I was hiding out?" Ben asked, sitting down beside Saul.

Bracken scratched his head. "Five, maybe six hours ride. Why?"

"Just thinking. You're wanting to keep clear of Preston. That would be a good place to go and I just might change my mind about telling you where that thirty thousand dollars is, once we were there."

The greed in Saul Bracken brought a glitter to his eyes. "You mean you'd just tell us where it was without expectin' us to make you no deal?"

Coe said, "Looks like Todd has made up his mind. But I still hate to think about that money not doing anybody some good. Kind of a sin, let it go to waste."

Saul Bracken swung about to his son. "Todd —" he began but the younger man cut him off.

"Forget it, Pa. That money ain't for us. Quit fooling yourself and quit listening to Duret. It's some kind of a trick."

The elder Bracken got to his feet and stalked away, muttering under his breath. Ben turned his attention to Laurie, working over the low fire. Her face was flushed from the heat and a stray lock of her dark hair hung over her forehead but she seemed not to notice. The odor of frying meat and potatoes was beginning to fill the clearing. He watched her set the pail of boiling water off the flames and add a generous handful of coffee to it. When it surged up to a foaming crest, she stirred it down with a knife.

Laying out four plates, she then portioned out the meal, reserving only a small amount in the frying pan for herself. Taking up one of the plates, she walked to where Ben sat and handed it to him.

Studying him gravely, she said: "You aren't Turk Duret. Who are you?"

CHAPTER
SEVENTEEN

There was a long, dead minute of silence. Time, itself, became a suspended thing. Ben returned Laurie's steady gaze, conscious of the thread of gladness that marked her tone. She had, somehow, recognized him and now remembered him from that night. But how?

"What did you say?" Todd Bracken broke the hush, his voice shocked and strained.

Laurie turned to her brother. "He's not Turk Duret. I don't know who he is but he's not Duret."

Orville Stelder had risen to his feet. Saul Bracken, scarcely pausing over his plate, scoffed. "Him not Duret? What are you sayin', girl? Didn't I see this same jasper in the courtroom with my own eyes?"

"He's the same man that was at the trial," Stelder confirmed. "I ain't wrong about that."

"Sure he is and for certain," Saul continued. He hesitated over his meal. "You gone and got yourself sot on this man, Laurie? I been suspectin' you was sweet on him ever since that mornin' when we stopped him and the marshal. Could see it in your eyes."

Orville Stelder swung a startled glance at Laurie and then looked down. Ben, too, stared at her, the words of old Saul Bracken filling him with a strange, powerful pride. But he said nothing; Todd Bracken, in his present state of mind, was unpredictable. The next few moments would be delicate, fraught with danger.

The younger Bracken moved up closer. "What kind of talk is that?" he snarled, pulling his gun and leveling it at Coe's breast. "You're the man I saw at the trial. You're the same one I jumped. You claim that's not so?"

The time had arrived. Marcelino Baca and his prisoner were on their own. Ben sighed his relief. "That's right. But my name's Coe. Ben Coe. I'm a deputy U.S. marshal."

Todd's face distorted as anger whipped through him. The hammer of his pistol clacked loudly as he drew it to a cocked position. Ben met the man's insane fury with a calmness he did not entirely feel and rode out the dragging moments. Laurie suddenly stepped before him, shielding his body with her own.

"No!" she said in a sharp voice. "You'll not kill him just because you've been outsmarted! You'll not have a murder on your hands!"

"Still don't believe it," Saul's plaintive voice broke the deadly tension. "I seen this here man right in the courtroom. You sayin' I didn't?"

"That was me," Ben explained, placing his hands on Laurie's shoulders and putting her gently aside. "I took Duret's place at the hearing. The real trial was held weeks ago in a different town. The law expected trouble from folks like you, and others, so I took his place. The real Duret is with Sheriff Baca, either in Capital City by now or almost there."

"You were a decoy, that it?" Stelder said, more as a statement than a question.

Ben nodded. But Todd Bracken was yet unconvinced. He continued to glare at Coe. The gun in his hand still pointed at the lawman. "I don't believe none of it," he said, finally.

"I can prove it," Laurie said at once. "I saw Ben — him. That night before the trial. I walked up to the hill behind our camp to look at the town. He rode up and stopped, coming from the river. He was just looking, too. When he scratched at that scar on his neck a while back, I knew I remembered something. Then it came to me; the man who was on the hill that night did the same thing. If he were Turk Duret, Todd, do you think he would just come riding in to Salvation of his own accord and turn himself in?"

Todd had no answer. Ben listened as Laurie went on telling about the two drunken cowboys, the fight that ensued. He grinned to himself. So that was how she knew — his scratching at that bullet track on his neck! A man's habits often prove his undoing and deliverance.

"Where's the real Duret?" Stelder asked.

"Probably in Capital City by now, as I said. Sheriff Baca left with him soon after Kilgore and I rode out of town. They took the valley road while we took this trail, hoping we would draw off any ambush."

"Damn you!" Todd Bracken suddenly cried in bitter, unreasonable anger and hurled himself at Ben. "I ought to kill you for tricking me!"

Coe stepped aside. As Todd came in, he struck him hard along the side of the head. The man went down to his knees, losing the gun as he did so. Ben scooped it up quickly and moved beyond Bracken's reaching hands.

"Tricking you!" Coe echoed. "You think I've enjoyed one minute of this? You people don't realize how important it is that Turk Duret gets hung in Capital City. It's not just the fact that it will get done there. There's more to it than that. Could be that statehood for this Territory depends on it." Ben paused, his own anger and impatience aroused.

"This hasn't been a job I liked, I'll tell you that. And it hasn't been a joke for me. You think I enjoyed the treatment I got from Preston and Waggoner? Or from you? I gambled my life on getting Duret to Capital City and Tom Kilgore, one of the best lawmen you'll ever live to see, gave his life for it! And you — you talk about killing me to satisfy your need for vengeance!"

"And I will!" Todd Bracken yelled and leaped again at Coe.

Ben whirled away from the lunging man. He had a fleeting glimpse of Laurie's horror-filled eyes; she fully expected him to shoot her brother, kill him. He brought the pistol down, clublike, on Todd's head. He went down full length and lay quiet.

Ben pivoted to Orville Stelder. "I don't want any trouble with you! Or you, Mr. Bracken. Both of you toss your guns out there on the ground. You, Orville, get a rope and tie Todd's hands behind him. I don't want to be dodging him all day."

Both men complied at once, Stelder procuring a short length of rope from his pocket and binding Todd Bracken's hands.

"The two of you sit down over there," Ben said, waving them to a position across the fire. "Need to think this out for a minute."

Laurie had stood quietly nearby. Her cheeks were colored from the excitement of the moments but she had said nothing. Ben faced her.

"I'm obliged to you," he said. "A friend is one thing I've been needing."

Saul Bracken grunted. "Reckon you got yourself more'n a friend, Marshal."

Laurie's cheeks flamed even brighter. She dropped to her knees beside the fire and poured coffee into the waiting cups. Ben squatted on his heels beside her.

"I hope," he said, softly, "what your pa said is true."

She hesitated a long moment and then turned to him. "Since that night along the trail — I've hoped we would meet again," she murmured. "I thought you had ridden on. I never dreamed it would end this way."

"There's no end," Coe said at once. "This is just the beginning. I had planned to come back this way and find you, after I was finished with my job, hoping that matters might work out for us. But I didn't even know if you would be interested. I feel now like I'm the luckiest man in the world."

Laurie's eyes were on the low fire. "But the way we treated you! The things we've said — can you forget all that?"

"They're forgotten," Ben said, laying his hand upon hers. "You thought I was Turk Duret."

From across the small clearing Saul Bracken asked, "What about this here Duret? You dead sure they'll string him up?"

"As certain as I'm here. You've got my solemn word on that."

Todd Bracken stirred, sat up. He struggled momentarily against his bonds and then glared at Coe.

"Ain't got much faith in them fancy-pants jaspers up there," old man Bracken said slowly. "Figure they'd just as soon let him go, would he tell them where he put that money, as not."

Ben Coe shook his head. "That's the wrong kind of thinking. Maybe it might have happened somewhere, sometime but it won't happen in Capital City. Turk Duret is as good as hung, right now."

"I'd believe that if I saw it," Todd Bracken said. "I got no reason to believe anything you're telling us."

"Up to you," Coe said, dismissing the argument. "But I'll be moving on to Capital City to wind up this job. Then I'll be coming back this way. Bring you any kind of proof you want."

Laurie's voice was a still, small sound in the quiet. "Then what will you do?"

"Go back to Kansas. That's where I work." Ben paused. "But before I do that, I'd like to tell you about Kansas. It's a fine place to live. Lots of people moving in. While I'm gone, would you think a little about going with me?"

118

She gave him a quick, sweet smile, her answer in her eyes. "I —"

There was the distinct crackle of a dry twig; the rustle of brush dragging lightly against cloth. It was off to the left, outside the clearing. Ben Coe came swiftly to his feet, his gun poised.

"What is it?" Laurie whispered, alarm stiffening her features.

"Somebody out there. Stand away from me."

Laurie moved back a step or two. The noise came again, much nearer. The forest about them was in absolute silence, no chirping birds, no clacking insects. But to Ben Coe the feel of danger was like a clanging bell.

"Nobody move!" a voice shattered the hush. "Preston — over here!"

Bill Ford's voice. Coe spun. In that same instant the outlaw fired. The bullet whirred past Coe, thunked into a tree behind Orville Stelder. Ben had a glimpse of the tall outline of Ford. He snapped a quick, answering shot. He heard the slug drive home, heard the gusty explosion of the outlaw's breath as it was smashed from his lungs.

Saul Bracken lunged for his gun. "Scatter!" he yelled. "Everybody scatter!"

CHAPTER
EIGHTEEN

There was then the racket of running horses — Preston and the others, summoned by Ford's shout were closing in.

"Bill! Bill Ford!" Waggoner's impatient voice rode through the quiet. "Where the devil are you?"

Ben reached for Laurie's hand. Saul Bracken and the others were moving off into the brush. "Come on," he said. "We've got to get out of here."

They slipped out of the clearing and into the thick undergrowth. They reached the horses. Ben freed Laurie's mare and the little white that had been provided for him. Taking the leathers, they hurried on, not mounting yet for fear their silhouettes might be more easily visible to Preston and his men.

Waggoner had ceased his yelling which could mean only one thing; he had found Bill Ford.

Ben drew the girl and their horses to the far side of a thickly overgrown osage orange. "I don't like this," he said. "I think the best thing is for you to wait here until some of your family shows up. I won't risk your getting hurt."

Laurie tipped her face to him. Her small chin was set stubbornly. "I'm going with you, no matter what."

"Before this is done with there is going to be some gunplay. That's a pretty wild bunch Preston's got with him and they won't care much who they shoot at."

"I've seen shooting before. And I'm not afraid of getting hit by a stray bullet. Anyway," she added, "if I'm to be the wife of a U.S. marshal, I might as well start getting used to such things."

Coe grinned in spite of the serious moment. He reached out, took her by the shoulders and planted a quick kiss upon her lips.

"All right, you win this hand," he said. "Now, let's get out of here."

Keeping low and still on foot, they left the shelter of the orange, headed straight away from the clearing where they had last encountered Preston and his riders. They were in single file with Coe leading but it was the girl who heard the first suspicious sound and murmured a warning.

"Ben! Off to the left! There's somebody."

Instantly Coe froze. The stop was too abrupt for the horses and there was a moment of confusion as they shied against the brush. Coe stepped quickly back to Laurie. He thrust his reins into her hand, warned her to silence with his eyes. He dropped back a few yards, faded into a stand of wild gooseberry. He had not yet heard the sound Laurie had caught. But it should be there, nearby. He took another few steps — and was face to face with Preston and the big rider, George Kemm.

"There he is —" Preston started. His words ended in a gasp as Coe hurled himself at the man, drove him flat to the ground. Kemm dropped the reins of the horse he was leading and lunged. Coe saw the move and rolled free of the banker. Kemm struck Preston and drove him back to the earth. Coe, up now and coming in fast, saw the cowboy clawing at his gun. He lashed out with a booted foot. His toe met the weapon, sent it spinning into the brush. He wanted no noise at this point. He could likely handle Kemm and C. J. Preston but Waggoner on his hands also would be too much. And a gunshot would bring the big rider quick.

"Get him!" Preston yelled at Kemm. He was pulling himself away from the center of action.

Coe, off balance from the kick he had delivered to Kemm's weapon, half fell. The cowboy grabbed at him, caught his leg. Coe fought to stay up but failed. He went down in a sprawling heap. Kemm swung at him, a long, roundhouse right delivered from a kneeling position. Coe ducked the slow traveling fist easily. He snatched at Kemm's arm, caught him by the wrist and jerked. The cowboy howled in pain as his shoulder wrenched.

Ben rolled to his feet. Movement behind him warned him of Preston. He lurched to one side just as the banker struck downward with a short length of wood. The limb caught him on the upper arm just above the elbow. The force of it sent pain shooting through his entire body but he knew it was momentary and not any serious injury. He wheeled then at Preston, a wild anger suddenly unleashed by the banker's blow. Preston yelled and tried to back away. He came up against

Kemm, tripped and both men went down in a flurry of arms and legs and muttered cursing.

Coe rushed in upon them. Time was getting away fast. The odds for their escape were growing less with each fleeting moment. He grasped the dazed Kemm by the shirt collar, half dragged him upright. Holding him, he drove his fist into the man's jaw. Kemm's head rolled and his body went limp. He spun to Preston but the banker was on his feet, scrambling for the brush ten feet away. Coe started to follow, thought better of it and ran quickly toward Laurie and the horses.

"Best trail north!" he said and swung to his saddle. "Lead out!"

Laurie rode off ahead of him, striking due west through the thick brush. He did not question her, knowing she was well acquainted with the country. He was more concerned with watching the trail behind them. But he saw no pursuers.

They soon broke out of the dense grove and onto a semi-open plains country. There was no road, only a long, shallow valley, lush with good grass. This continued for a mile or so and then led into a narrow wash that one time flood water had grooved during its rushing descent from the high hills. Travel became more difficult at that point and the horses were compelled to take things slower. But they were well hidden. Only a man riding directly into the narrow slash could know of their whereabouts.

An hour later they reached the same trail that Coe had covered that previous day with Waggoner and his bogus soldiers.

"This is the road to Capital City," Laurie said. "You think it's safe to ride it or do we keep to the brush?"

Ben considered. Preston and his outlaws were behind them and to the east; they were the only problem. And they needed to travel fast.

"Let's stick to the main road," Coe said finally. "Right now we need to put a few miles between Preston and ourselves."

Around noon, with the horses showing the effects of the steady pace, they drew off the trail into a narrow wash. There, in the shade of a small cottonwood, they halted for a rest. It was a dry camp. There was no water for either the horses or themselves but just being out of the saddle was good. Ben eased the animals by loosening their cinches.

When he was finished, he sat down beside Laurie. He was still finding it hard to believe she was with him, was willing to have him, and go to Kansas with him.

"Laurie," he said, taking her hand in his. "I don't want you doing something you might later be sorry for. You made up your mind pretty fast back there in the camp. If you think now you'd like to wait a spell, it will be all right with me."

Laurie turned to him, studied his grave face for a long moment. Then, leaning forward, she kissed him on the lips.

"You men are such fools!" she said with a smile. "You seem to think love is a one-sided business. Don't you think I was as sure back there of what I wanted — as you were? What has time to do with how much a woman loves a man? I suppose there are cases where

124

two people can learn to care for one another. A sort of a gradual thing, I guess you might call it, and there's nothing wrong with that. But I think the best kind is the kind where you know instantly that you have met the person you love. That was the way of it with me, Ben."

Coe nodded. "And with me, Laurie. I never got you out of my thoughts after that first meeting."

He put his arm about her slim shoulders, drew her against him. "Be glad when this job is done with. Then we can start living like people should. Right now," he added, kissing her lightly and releasing her, "I expect we ought to travel. No use pressing our luck too far."

"Your luck," Tibo Waggoner's deliberate voice reached out from the brush and shocked them, "just run clean out, Duret. Now, don't make 'no sudden moves. Just stand up with your hands stuck out where I can see them."

Ben got slowly to his feet, anger at his own carelessness raging through him. He should have guessed one of the outlaws, at least, would have spotted Laurie and him traveling northward. He should have used more care, he reflected bitterly. Now, he had dragged Laurie into his own troubles.

"Step out here into the open," Waggoner said. The outlaw moved from the brush into the small clearing, as he spoke. He watched Ben comply. "Soon as that horse of mine gets his breath, we'll all ride back to Preston and the boys. Didn't get no chance to tell them I saw you two ridin' north. They're still beatin' the brush back there in that grove."

Waggoner was alone. Ben realized that and a faint spark of hope began to glow within him. He half turned his head to look at Laurie. She was standing several paces behind him.

"Reckon I better have that gun you're wearin'," Waggoner said. "Take it out, easy like, and toss it on the ground here, in front of me."

Coe gauged his chances. He had one and one only. It was slim but it might work. He glanced again at Laurie, assuring himself she was not in the line of Waggoner's gun. Satisfied, he lowered his hand slowly over the butt of his pistol.

"Don't get no notions," Waggoner warned.

Coe's expression did not change. His eyes were locked with those of the outlaw. He felt the curved handle of the gun fit up into his palm. He let his fingers close about the smooth wood. Slowly he began to lift the weapon, letting Waggoner see every move.

"Throw it down," the outlaw said, a frown pulling his thick brows together.

"Sure," Coe answered. "Just like you want it."

He brought the gun out. Holding it loosely, he started a forward motion with his arm. In the next fleeting fragment of time, he was hurling himself to one side and to the ground. Waggoner's gun blasted in unison with his own. Ben felt the bullet rip through the cloth of his shirt. He fired again, seeing the outlaw's upright shape still before him. It was a wasted shot. Waggoner, hit in the chest, was staring at him with wonder-filled eyes. He seemed more surprised than hurt. The second bullet jolted him, rocked him back a

126

step. He wavered uncertainly for a long moment. The pistol slipped from his hand and then he fell heavily, going down into the brush at the edge of the clearing.

Ben was on his feet instantly. Laurie ran to him, her eyes anxious. But she asked no questions. She saw he was all right and that was the answer she sought.

"We've got to get out of here," Coe said, wheeling to where the horses waited. "Likely, somebody will have heard those shots."

He pulled the cinches tight and they mounted up. Riding quickly out of the draw, they came to the road.

"This time," he said, "we better keep to the brush. My guess is we'll have company right soon."

CHAPTER
NINETEEN

The brief rest had benefited the horses. They moved along through the hindering brush and scrubby trees at a good pace, slowing up only when they came on to a rocky slope where the footing was more difficult. Ben did not let up until a full hour had passed. Then he called a halt.

He dismounted and moved to a low hill that overlooked the trail behind them. Laurie joined him there and together they sat quietly, listening and watching for signs of pursuit. At first there was no evidence the shots had been heard. Then they heard the distinct rap of fast running horses. The sound was far to the east which could mean only one thing; the riders, whoever they were, had taken the valley road, were following the more open route for the sake of speed.

"Preston?" Laurie asked, alarm in her tone.

Coe nodded. "Can't figure what he's doing over there. Thought he would come swarming up to where the gunshots were. Unless . . ." he added thoughtfully and hesitated.

"Unless what?"

"Unless he's got some sort of idea to circle around ahead of us, cut us off."

Laurie said nothing. Fear for Ben was plain in her eyes. She looked away. "Wouldn't it just be better to face Preston, make him understand you're not Turk Duret but a U.S. marshal? Maybe if he knew that he would forget about trying to capture you."

Ben placed his arm about her shoulders. "You think I could make him believe that? Waggoner still thought I was Duret and I'm not even sure I've got your own brother and father convinced. Or Orville. Preston is going to believe what he saw — me in that courtroom on trial for killing your brother's wife and child. Trying to tell him he's wrong would be a waste of time. I will first have to have proof of some kind."

She shrugged wearily. "I suppose you're right. But it all seems so useless, so unnecessary. You might even get killed just because you can't prove who you really are."

"That was the idea behind this whole set-up. Make everybody believe I was someone I wasn't. At least up to a certain point. Then Tom Kilgore was to step in and clear it all up."

"Only Tom Kilgore is dead," she finished, "and there's nobody to straighten matters out, not until you get back to Salvation and see the judge. Ben, this could cost you your life."

He said, "My job, Laurie," and stopped. After a moment he added, "But it's not quite as bad as you think. It will come out all right. Once we reach Capital City it will all be over with. Sheriff Baca will be there to verify my story. And so will the prison officials. I don't know them but they can easily clear me."

"If we ever reach Capital City."

"We will, don't worry about that."

"I hope so, Ben. I pray nothing will happen to you. I — I don't think I could go on living now if anything happened to you. I wouldn't want to."

"You worry too much," he said with a broad grin.

She said, "I guess you're right. What do we do?"

"Go on, of course. Finish the job. Unless I'm wrong that's only two horses. Preston and Kemm. Maybe three if Conley's along. Might be some others back along the trail, just waiting for us. That way they've got us pocketed."

"I see," she murmured. "Either way we go, we're trapped."

He grinned at her, trying to ease her worry. "Not all over yet. One thing to set up a trap, another thing to spring it. Best thing we can do, I figure, is keep moving for Capital City."

Near the middle of the afternoon, with their horses pulled down to a steady walk, they drew near the end of the mountain range, a long, trailing backbone which sloped down until it disappeared into a far reaching mesa. Coe, probing it carefully, was aware of one thing; once they left the brush and protective shadows of the hills, they would be out in the open, flat ground. They would be easily seen in all directions, for a considerable distance.

"Any idea how far to Capital City from here?" he asked Laurie, thinking she might be familiar with the area.

The girl shook her head. "I'm not sure. I've never been there. But I think it's twenty or thirty miles."

130

"Lot of open range to cross," he said, voicing his thoughts. He glanced to the sun. "Quite a while until dark and hate to waste that time. Think we'll just pull up there in that grove and rest the horses for a bit and then move on." He did not explain that he wanted the animals in the best possible condition when they started across the flat mesa; there was every possibility they might have to make a run for it.

They continued on and a short time later reached the scatter of trees, all thick-bodied cottonwoods clustered about a small spring. As they approached, a horseman suddenly appeared and rode forward to meet them. Ben Coe's hand dropped to the gun at his hip but Laurie's voice stayed him.

"It's Papa. It's my father!"

Saul Bracken trotted his gray up beside them. "Had me a mite worried," he said, mopping sweat off his brow with the back of a hairy wrist. "All that shootin' back there. Figured maybe you was in trouble."

"Waggoner," Coe said. "That you we heard coming up the valley?"

Bracken nodded. "Reckon so. Todd and me figured to catch up and ride into Capital City with you. Got a hankerin' to see Duret hang, ourselves. That way we'll know the job's been done."

"Where's Todd?" Laurie asked, looking about.

"Settin' over there in the shade. Got hisself nicked by a bullet."

"Todd's been shot?" Laurie exclaimed.

"Not bad. One of Preston's bunch."

"Where's Orville? He didn't get . . ." Laurie faltered.

"Kilt? Nope. Orvie's all right. Last time I saw him he was tearin' off through the brush with one of Preston's buckos on his tail. Expect he led the feller down the valley a ways and then went on home."

Ben was thinking deeply. Since it had been the Brackens they had heard, Preston and his men must be behind them yet. Coming up the trail, most likely. It meant one thing: they would have to forego the proposed rest for the horses. They would have to push on at once. It would not pay to let Preston get too close.

They entered the shadows of the grove and pulled up beside the spring. Todd Bracken, a handkerchief wrapped about his left forearm, was sitting with his back propped against a tree. He watched Ben with a cold hostility and gave no greeting to Laurie as she dismounted and hurried to his side.

"How bad is it, Todd?" she asked, her fingers plucking at the stained cloth.

Todd brushed her roughly aside. "Forget it."

Saul Bracken said, "Todd still ain't so sure about you, Coe. One of the reasons why we decided we'd just go on into Capital City. They don't hang Duret, then we got us a mighty big bone to pick with you."

Todd, never changing his hot, hating glance from Ben said to Laurie, "You're a fool to be believing so strong in this man. Maybe he's not Duret but I won't even bet for sure on that. And if he ain't, he's in with those other jaspers in Capital City that's running this Territory. And he'll sell us out just like they're planning to do."

132

"You're wrong, Todd," the girl said. "I wish I could make you see it but you're all wrong. Ben isn't in with anybody, as you claim. He is just a lawman doing the job that was assigned to him. I believe that. And when he tells me the real Duret is being delivered to Capital City for hanging, I believe that, too."

Todd spat in disgust. "Sure, he can make you swallow anything he says. He's the kind who can sweet talk a woman into anything. You really think he means all those things he's been telling you — maybe about marrying up and such?"

Laurie made no reply. She stared at her hands.

"He's just using you as his ticket to get to Capital City. Once he's there, you'll see. He'll drop you like a hot potato, leave you flat. I know his kind."

Laurie shook her head. "I believe him, Todd."

Ben Coe, anger steadily rising within him, crossed to the younger Bracken. "You all through?" he demanded in a tight, outraged voice. "You weren't Laurie's brother and crippled up, I'd make you eat those words, Todd! I'd take a lot of pleasure in kicking your teeth in. And when this is all finished, I'm making a special trip back down here to do just that."

Todd returned his furious gaze. "You'll never live that long, Duret. I'll kill you before you get a chance to start back."

A sudden wild fury blazed through Ben Coe. "Of all the bull-headed, knot-brained —" he began, taking a long step toward the man. Laurie came to her feet at once, threw herself before him.

"It doesn't matter, Ben," she said in a low, soothing voice. "What he or anybody else says doesn't matter to me. I believe what you say."

Ben turned away, his arm going around the girl. She was right. No matter what Todd or anyone else thought, it was of no consequence. Just so long as Laurie had faith in him. He had his hands about her shoulders, holding her before him, looking down at her. He heard then the harsh voice of C. J. Preston lash out from the brush behind him.

"Put your hands up, Duret! You're covered!"

CHAPTER
TWENTY

Coe moved gently away from Laurie. He let his hands remain poised, only half lifted. Saul Bracken had come to his feet but Todd had not moved. Ben gauged the approximate location of Preston; almost directly behind him, he figured. If he could get another two steps to the left of Laurie, thus removing her from the line of fire, he could whirl, drop and shoot. And maybe bring to a close, once and for all, this problem he had with C. J. Preston. In the next moment he knew such was out of the question.

George Kemm's voice, coming from the other side of the clearing reached out to him. "Duret, if you're gettin' one of your cute ideas, forget it. I've got you covered, too."

Coe came to a stop. He was trapped between the two men. He might get one but never the pair of them.

"Just stand quiet," Preston said. "And raise those hands higher! Turn around slow."

Ben complied. He had no choice. He came slowly about.

"Don't none of the rest of you folks get any ideas either. Now!" he added, glancing at the Brackens. They did as they were ordered.

"You ain't got no right to do this!" Saul Bracken protested, suddenly finding his voice.

Preston laughed. He moved further into the center of the clearing. "Old man, I got thirty thousand rights —"

"But he's not Turk Duret!" Laurie broke in, rushing to Coe's side. "He's not the man you want. He's a lawman, a deputy U.S. marshal. He was only taking Duret's place."

The words poured out in a breathless torrent. Preston listened, faint humor in his eyes. When Laurie had finished he said, "I suppose you'll be telling me next that he isn't the man I saw in the courtroom back in Salvation. That he's not the one I saw marched in by the marshal and sheriff and then taken out after Abraham sentenced him to hang."

"Yes, but —" Laurie began, floundering with her words. "He's the man all right but he's not Duret. He —"

Preston turned his back to her. He faced Kemm. "Get some rope, George. We're going to work this a little different this time. We don't have Tibo to help us loosen Duret's tongue but I figure if we drag him along behind a horse for a mile or two he might be ready to talk."

"You can't!" Laurie cried. "You can't do that to him! He's not Turk Duret! I swear it!"

Laurie threw herself upon Ben Coe as if to shield him from the two men. Kemm grasped her by the shoulders and roughly shoved her at Saul Bracken.

"She's your kin," he said. "Keep her out of the way unless you want her to get hurt."

136

Todd Bracken had risen to his feet. He moved into the middle of the cleared area and faced Preston. "There any doubt in your mind who this man is?" he asked, pointing at Coe.

Preston said, "Hell, no. Why should there be? I saw him before with my own eyes. Anybody that says he's not that same man is loony."

Todd Bracken nodded his satisfaction. "Way I've felt all the time but that sister of mine claims he's somebody else."

"Who?"

"Somebody by the name of Ben Coe. A deputy U.S. marshal, she says."

Preston shrugged. "That doesn't make sense. Kilgore was the marshal on this case. Why would he have a deputy, too? Lawmen aren't that plentiful."

Todd Bracken considered that statement, his face immediately showing his belief. He swung to Coe.

"You still claim you're not Duret?"

"I'm not Duret," Ben replied coldly. "And anything you do to me you'll answer to the United States government for. Now, turn me loose."

"He's a real hard talker, ain't he?" Kemm said, uncoiling the rope he had procured from his saddle. "How you want to do this, Mr. Preston?"

"Tie his hands behind him. Then loop that rope around his middle. Tie the other end to your saddle horn."

"No!" Laurie moaned and broke free of her father.

Todd caught her by the arm, whirled her about and sent her stumbling back to the elder Bracken. "Hang

137

onto her, Pa. We'll tie her up, too, if she keeps on making a fuss. Ain't no doubt in my mind now about this being Turk Duret. How about you?"

Saul Bracken wagged his head. "I surely don't know what I'm thinkin'," he muttered helplessly.

"He's not Turk Duret," Laurie said, her words ending in a sob. "You will be murdering the wrong man."

"Maybe not murder," Preston said. "Maybe he'll be smart enough this time to answer my question. He does that, he won't get hurt."

Todd Bracken said, "Mr. Preston, we both been after the same man but for different reasons. You want to get your money back. I want the pure pleasure of stringing him up to a tree limb. No use of us fighting over him."

Preston said, "That's right."

"Suppose we sort of join up. I'll help you find out what you want to know. Then you turn him over to me, so's I can do what I got to do."

Preston thought for a time. He nodded. "Sounds all right to me. Don't figure I need any help, way this is working out, but if you want to throw in with me, I'm agreeable. When I'm finished with him, he's all yours."

Ben Coe had listened to the conversation in silence. They were taking good care of him, he thought grimly. Carving him up like a Christmas turkey. And when they were done there would be nothing left. Nothing but a body swinging from a tree for the buzzards to have their time with. He glanced to Laurie. Her father had a firm grasp upon her wrist, keeping her at his side. He was sorry she was to be a witness to the next few hours.

138

Saul Bracken should take her and head back to Salvation. No sense in her being put through the torture he soon would be undergoing. He felt Kemm jerk at his hands, draw them down behind his back.

"Here's a strip of rawhide," Todd Bracken volunteered. "Tie his wrists with it and he won't be working loose."

His last minutes of life were facing him. Ben Coe recognized that fact. A desperate anger lifted suddenly within him. He wasn't giving in this easy! Once his hands were bound, he would have little if any chance at all remaining. Better to try now and perhaps go down under a bullet than wait and endure the tender mercies of C. J. Preston — with only Todd Bracken's lynch rope waiting for him if he managed to survive that! He drew himself taut, considering his best course of action. He felt Kemm tug at his hands, pulling them away from his body so that he might more easily wrap the rawhide about his wrists.

In that instant he acted. He threw himself back against Kemm. The sheer weight of his body knocked the man against the low brush. He tripped, went down. Coe wheeled and ducked aside, knowing Preston would shoot. The gun exploded but the bullet was wide. Coe drove forward into Preston. His shoulder caught the man in the midsection. Preston's breath went out in a blast. He buckled, his pistol blasting a second time.

Coe spun away. Kemm, recovered, was coming back into the clearing, curses streaming from his thick lips. Ben wheeled to face him. He was vaguely conscious of Laurie's scream, of a dark shape moving in upon him from the side. Todd! He had ignored the man, knowing he was unarmed and had concentrated on Kemm and Preston. Laurie screamed again just as Kemm lunged at him. Something crashed down upon his head. Lights spun before his eyes and he went to his knees.

"Don't, Todd!"

He heard Laurie's voice, realized it was Todd who had hit him with a club or a rock or something solid. He saw the grinning face of George Kemm before him, felt a warm stickiness on his head. He went forward to his hands, struggling to keep from going clear down. He saw Kemm's boot rise to meet him. The shock of the impact against his jaw drove him over backwards.

He lay quiet only barely conscious. The effort to move was more than he could muster at the moment. There was no feeling in his long body, no strength. Faintly he heard Preston's voice.

"Let him be. He won't try it again. Get some water from the spring, George."

A minute later cold water dashed against his face and yanked his senses out of the fog. He gasped, came to a sitting position. Kemm and Todd Bracken took him under the armpits and jerked him to his feet. He stood there, weaving uncertainly, his brain clearing. He could hear Laurie crying brokenly, could feel the warmness of blood trickling through his scalp, down the side of his face. Why didn't Saul Bracken take Laurie away? Why was he allowing her to see all this?

Kemm clamped his hands together, bound them tight with the rawhide. He walked around to face Coe.

140

He grinned, his broad teeth yellow and large as those of a horse.

"Now, bucko, let's see you try that again," he said and drove his fist into Coe's unprotected belly.

Ben folded, his head spinning as pain shattered his nerves again. He staggered and almost fell. Todd Bracken caught him and held him upright.

Preston said, "No more of that, George! I want him able to talk. You're bad as Tibo."

"Owed him that one," Kemm replied.

"And I got to have him alive to string —" Todd Bracken began and then abruptly stopped.

Coe lifted his eyes to the man wondering what had checked him. Bracken, as did all the others, looked beyond him towards the edge of the clearing.

A strange voice said, "Now, just what kind of a party we got goin' here?"

Ben turned slowly around. Three hard-faced men with drawn guns stood just outside the ring of brush. A single word jarred involuntarily from his lips.

"Duret!"

CHAPTER
TWENTY-ONE

There was no mistaking the heavy, brutal features of the man. Ben had seen him back in the jail at Salvation, asleep on a cot. There was no doubt. Somehow the killer had escaped Marcelino Baca, probably with the help of the two men with him. And most likely the sheriff was at that moment lying dead along the trail, victim of an ambush.

Duret and his companions moved into the clearing. Each carried a pistol in his hand. Their cartridge belts were completely filled. It apparently had been a well planned rescue. Kilgore and Frank Abraham had labored for nothing. And Kilgore was dead, and probably Baca.

"Looks like they been treatin' you a mite rough, *amigo*," Duret said easily, halting before Coe. "What they got against you?"

Ben Coe thought fast. He realized he was the last hope for getting Duret to Capital City and the justice he deserved. Just how it could yet be done was not clear but so long as he was himself alive, he must try. Perhaps, if he could persuade Duret they were of the same breed, of the same mind.

He said, "Seems quite a few things. Was about to become the main party in a hanging bee when you showed up."

Duret nodded. "So I see." His gaze was going beyond Coe, resting on Laurie.

"Obliged to you for stepping in," Ben said. "How about cutting me loose? Rawhide's pulled pretty tight."

"Sure," Duret said. "Cut him loose, Earl."

One of the men stepped forward. He drew a knife from his pocket and sliced through the thong.

Preston, recovered from his surprise, said, "You — you're Turk Duret?"

The outlaw swung his attention to the banker, having his moment of pride at being recognized. "That's me."

"Then who's this man?" Preston exclaimed, plainly confused as he pointed at Coe.

Duret swung his narrow, sardonic face to Ben. "You been tellin' folks around here you're Turk Duret, *amigo*?"

"They've been telling me that," Coe said honestly. "I've been trying to convince them that I'm not."

"Who are you? I know you?"

Ben shook his head. "Don't think so. Name is Coe."

"Claims he's a U.S. marshal," Saul Bracken broke in. "A deputy, anyway."

Duret stared at Coe. He grinned. "Man, you sure do swap around some! Now, even I know better than that. Only one U. S. marshal around here. Name is Kilgore and I'm mighty well acquainted with him. Ain't I, Earl?" he added, glancing at one of his partners.

Earl laughed. "And the sheriff, too."

143

"Who might you be?" Duret continued, turning his attention to Preston.

"I'm C. J. Preston. I own the bank you robbed."

Duret sucked at his lips thoughtfully. "What's that got to do with this *amigo* of mine, Coe?"

"We thought he was Duret — you."

"And you figured to make him cough up that thirty thousand dollars I stashed away, that it?"

Preston said, "Yes, that's it. But now that I know he's not, I'm ready to make a deal with you."

Duret stared at the banker, shook his head admiringly. "You sure have got a crust, I'll say that for you. Why would I be wanting to make a deal with you?"

"You still have to get out of the country. I could help you do that."

"I don't need no help," Duret said flatly and switched his attention to Todd. "Who are you, mister?"

Todd Bracken's face was a ghostly white. His eyes were spread wide and his mouth worked convulsively. "You murdered my wife, my baby," he began and suddenly lunged for Duret. A long-blade knife glittered in his hand.

Ben, standing beside the outlaw, moved fast. He struck out with his fist, caught Todd on the shoulder. It knocked Bracken off balance. Following up quickly, Ben drove another blow into Todd's jaw. Todd reeled off, fell heavily into the brush.

Duret stared at him in silence. Finally he said, "The husband, that it? Reckon he had a call comin'. But you keep a eye on him, Earl. He makes another move like that, kill him."

144

He came back to Coe. "You're a mighty handy boy to have around, *amigo. Muchas gracias.*"

"We better be moving on, Turk," Earl spoke up then. "Liable to be a posse riding our tail by now."

"Sure, sure," Duret said. His glance was again upon Laurie. "Ain't met everybody here yet. Like that little filly there."

"Forget her," Earl said quickly. "Woman got you caught the last time. Let's don't be asking for it again."

"You're too scary, Earl. Might be worth the risk."

Saul Bracken bristled. He took a step forward. "Leave her be," he said, his voice different, strong and threatening. "She's my daughter. You'll have to kill me afore you can lay a hand on her!"

Duret shrugged, clearly unimpressed. The moments were growing critical — and Laurie was in great danger. A harsh fear clutched at Ben Coe as he recalled the terrible fate that had befallen Todd Bracken's wife.

He said, "Turk, we ought to be pulling out of here. There's a posse, a different one, loose around here somewhere. Looking for me. They might stumble on to us if we stay around much longer."

Duret's flat eyes swiveled restlessly to him. "Reckon maybe you're right, *amigo.* You figure to ride with us?"

Coe said, "What I had in mind."

"How far?"

"Mexico. For a spell, anyway. Soon as things cool off, thought I'd drop back over into Arizona Territory. Nobody knows me there."

Duret said, "Good enough. Only you're on your own. You understand that?"

"Sure," Ben said. He was watching Laurie. He saw the disbelief and shock crowd into her eyes. From the edge of the clearing Todd spoke up.

"What did I tell you, Laurie? Didn't I tell you right about him?" There was a note of triumph in his voice.

Laurie met Ben's gaze. She stared at him for a long moment and then he saw the light go out of her eyes. She lowered her face, turned away from him. If only he could tell her the truth! That he was only pretending to go along with Duret, long enough to win his confidence and allow him to effect a recapture. But there was no way, no time. She would believe Todd was right.

"You got a gun?" Turk's voice asked.

He nodded woodenly. He walked to the brush where Kemm had tossed it. Recovering it, he thrust it into his holster.

"We just going to leave all these people here, standing around?" Earl asked. "Kind of risky if there's a posse off there in the woods."

"Reckon we had ought to shut them up," Duret said with no apparent qualms.

"Gunshots would be heard," Coe put in hurriedly. "Bring that posse down on us fast. How about just tying them up? Couldn't do any harm, that way."

Duret nodded. "Good idea. You boys get busy."

Earl took the rope Kemm had brought in earlier to use on Coe. He cut it into shorter lengths and handed some to Coe and some to the third outlaw who had stood silently by during all the conversation. They began at once to bind the Brackens, Preston and

146

Kemm. Coe managed to work his way to Laurie. He looped the rope about her wrists, not pulling it tight.

"Laurie, you've got to believe me," he said in a low whisper. "I have to do it this way. Trust me."

She did not look at him. Saul Bracken glared up into his face. "You dirty sneak!" he said. "I should have believed my boy! He knew what he was talkin' about. Maybe you wasn't Turk Duret but you're sure one of his bunch."

Ben ignored the old man's acid words. "Laurie, please listen . . ."

"Let's get out of here," Duret said. "Come on, Coe, if you're ridin' with us."

"Good-bye, Laurie," Ben whispered. But she did not look up or make any reply.

They rode away from the clearing, the sound of Todd Bracken's curses ringing in their ears. Duret glancing back, shrugged.

"I had the time, I'd go back and shut that jaybird up with a bullet. Put him out of his misery."

"He's sure got hisself a powerful hate for you," Earl observed.

"Guess he has a right," Duret answered. He turned to Ben, riding a step back and to one side. "You any idea where that posse might be, cowboy?"

Coe made a show of thinking about that. Finally, "Figure we would be better off over in the valley. They've been through there. If they're keeping an eye on this trail we'll be spotted sooner or later."

Duret said nothing but immediately swung his horse sharp left and slanted for the valley. The others followed, Ben still bringing up the rear. They traveled another mile and began to enter the heavier timber.

"Saw you talkin' to that little filly back there, Coe," Duret said. "That what all the ruckus was about? Her pa maybe didn't cotton the idea of you two?"

"Little like that," Ben answered.

He was watching the third man narrowly, alert for the first opportunity that would present itself. He could not afford a shootout with them. He would have small chance against their combined guns. And he did not want Duret killed. The outlaw had to live to hang. Tom Kilgore had given his life for that. And Marcelino Baca, too. For those reasons he could take no chances on losing his own life. He must stay alive to deliver Turk Duret.

They reached the grove, far enough now from the Brackens and Preston to make a move. Ahead of him the outlaws dropped into a single file as the trail narrowed because of the thick underbrush. The man called Earl was in the lead. He was followed by Duret after whom came the third outlaw, his name still unknown. Coe brought up the rear. The going became slower as the trail grew more confined. Ben could see no possibility of moving up quietly, getting the third man out of the way and capturing Turk Duret. And then quite suddenly opportunity presented itself.

They reached a wide place in the trail. Duret pulled off to the side, allowed the third outlaw to pass him by. He waited for Ben.

"Coe," he said, kneeing his horse in beside Ben's, "you know this country pretty well?"

148

Ben, his eyes on the backs of the two other outlaws, now several yards ahead, nodded. He came to a halt.

"What's up?" Duret asked, pulling in.

"Horse picked up a rock, I think." He examined the horse's hoof. "Guess not," he said several minutes later and swung back into the saddle. The two outlaws were well out of sight, beyond a bend in the trail.

"What did you ask me? Did I know this country?"

Duret said, "Yeh. Do you?"

"Like the back of my hand," Coe said, lying generously. "Why?"

"Well, got a little business to tend to when we get close to a town they call Salvation. Then I want to get into Mexico, quickest way."

"I know the road," Ben said.

"You get me there fast and I'll make it worth your while."

"We got a deal," Ben said and waited for Duret to move by him and resume his place on the trail. He watched the outlaw go by. When he was an arm's length past, he drew his gun. He brought it down hard on the outlaw's skull. Duret grunted and doubled forward in his saddle.

Coe acted quickly. He jerked off his neckerchief, bound it around the outlaw's mouth, effectively gagging him. He took a short length of soft rope that he found in the gray's saddle-bags, and tied the outlaw's hands securely behind his back.

"Hey, Turk?" Earl's call came from farther along the trail.

"We're coming! Coe shouted back. "Keep going."

He took up the reins of Duret's horse and turned about. He threw a glance to the south, to where Earl and the third man were. There was no sign of them. They, evidently, were still beyond the bend. With Duret yet unconscious, Coe started up the valley, towing the outlaw's horse behind him. If he could get a little distance between themselves and the others before they became suspicious, he might avoid a fight.

He had scarcely got that thought out of his mind when he heard them pounding up behind him. He glanced over his shoulder. They were rounding the bend, Earl in the lead, the other man not far back of him. They were coming on fast. Duret groaned and stirred in the saddle. Coe saw then a widening in the trail, a small clearing where an upthrusting of rock formed a solid shoulder. He reached it, drew quickly off to the side.

He dismounted, stepped to Duret's horse. Taking the outlaw's pistol he stuck it into his own belt after which he tied both horses securely to a stout cedar growing near the edge of the rock. This done he moved back to the trail. Earl and his partner, suspicious, had halted. They waited a few yards distant. With a gun in either hand, Coe stepped boldly out into the center of the trail.

"I'm a U.S. deputy marshal," he called out. "I'm taking Turk Duret back to Capital City to hang. I'm giving you a warning now. You try and stop me and I'll kill you. Both of you!"

Earl half turned in his saddle, threw a smirking glance at the other man. "Well, now, lawman, maybe

150

you will and maybe you won't," he said and reached for his pistol.

Coe threw himself to one side, fired both guns fast. One of the bullets caught Earl in the chest. He went out of the saddle and fell heavily to the ground. Ben, his guns now lined on the third man, waited.

"How about it?"

The outlaw raised his hands slowly, carefully, over his head. "Not for me, Marshal," he drawled. "Was just along for the ride. Run into that pair up the road a few miles. Once knew Duret."

"You with Earl when he helped spring Duret from the sheriff?"

"Nope. That was Earl and some other waddy. He caught himself a bullet, I hear." He stopped, added, "I don't want no truck with the law. If it's all same to you, I'll just mosey along."

"Maybe what you're telling me is true and maybe it's not. But I don't have time to fool around with it now. What's your name?"

"Bass. Friends call me Sam."

"All right, Sam Bass. Ride on and keep riding. Don't look back."

"Yes, sir," the cowboy said. He wheeled about and started down the trail.

Coe watched him until he was out of sight. He loaded the dead outlaw onto his horse, secured the body and returned to where Duret, now angrily conscious, waited. The outlaw greeted him with a scowling hatred and a thorough cursing but Coe ignored the man. There was one thing yet to be sure of

— Sam Bass. He climbed to the top of the rock and turned his eyes to the south. Minutes later he saw a rider, little more than a speck, in the long distance. Bass had done as he had been ordered; he had kept on riding.

With a sigh Coe returned to his horse. He climbed into the saddle, motioned Duret to pull out ahead of him. With Earl's horse bringing up the rear, they started off. It would be a hard ride to Capital City.

CHAPTER
TWENTY-TWO

They hanged Turk Duret for his crimes that next day at high noon.

It took place within the high walls of the Territorial prison on a new, well constructed gallows. It was true the execution was witnessed by only a few but word of the outlaw's death at the firm hands of the law would spread quickly throughout the country. Before another day had passed, the knowledge would be well established that a just law now existed.

It had cost the lives of two fine lawmen, Kilgore and Marcelino Baca. But the victory was won and there now was small question of statehood. Ben Coe, shaved, rested and dressed in clean clothing, swung up to the saddle and rode slowly for the iron grillwork gate in the south wall of the yard. Kansas was a long way off. And it would be a lonely ride.

Never before had his solitary travels been a burden to him. Indeed, he had preferred it that way, going and coming as fancy suited him or the job required. It was different now. He had to continually resist the urge to glance sidewards, to see if Laurie Bracken were not at his elbow. Strange how those few, short hours with her had so completely altered his life.

But Laurie had made her decision; she had been faced with a difficult choice and had made it. He did not blame her for it, only himself for not making it easier for her. Trouble was, there had been no time. Things had happened so fast. If he could have talked with her, made her understand his side of it.

"*Adios*, Marshal," the gatekeeper called, swinging back the lace ironwork. "*Hasta la vista*."

Ben nodded and thought, *not likely*. Chances were he never again would be in Capital City. His job lay in Kansas and besides, there were too many memories left here to plague him. He would never again look at a towering, shadowed mountain or across the broad fling of a mesa without thinking of her.

He turned his new horse, a long-legged bay, onto the east road, towards home. He pulled up short. A hundred yards off to the right three riders waited in the shade of an apricot tree. As he watched, one of them separated from the others and hurried to meet him.

Laurie!

She was smiling and Ben Coe realized at once that he had been wrong, that he had underestimated her love for him, that his own faith and trust in her had fallen short.

"What's the trouble, Marshal?" the gatekeeper called after him. "Lose somethin'?"

"Yes," Ben answered, "but I just found it."

He spurred the bay forward to meet her.